A VOW OF VENGEANCE!

Eddie Brock and Venom knew more about Spider-Man than almost anyone alive. They knew where he lived, they knew where he worked.

They knew his secret identity.

We are getting better able to control ourselves, Venom thought.

Another time they would have leapt down in front of everyone to rip out Spider-Man's spleen. Now the rage was cold in Venom's gut, colder than the lashing snow.

"We will destroy you," Venom whispered. "You stole our lives, and now you take credit for our deeds. We will destroy you in both of your guises. Spider-Man and Peter Parker will know what it is to steal from Venom!"

MIDNIGHT JUSTICE

Martin Delrio

Illustrations by Neil Vokes
& Michael Avon Oeming

BYRON PREISS MULTIMEDIA COMPANY, INC.
NEW YORK

POCKET BOOKS
New York London Toronto Sydney Tokyo Singapore

An *Original* Publication of POCKET BOOKS

POCKET BOOKS, a division of Simon & Schuster Inc.
1230 Avenue of the Americas, New York, NY 10020

Byron Preiss Multimedia Company, Inc.
24 West 25th Street
New York, New York 10010

The Byron Preiss Multimedia Worldwide Web Site Address is:
http://www.byronpreiss.com

ISBN: 0-671-57851-5

First Pocket Books paperback printing April 1996

10 9 8 7 6 5 4 3 2 1

POCKET and colophon are registered trademarks of
Simon & Schuster Inc.

Edited by Howard Zimmerman
Cover art by Mike Zeck and Phil Zimelman
Cover design by Claude Goodwin
Interior design by MM Design 2000, Inc.

Printed in the U.S.A.

PROLOGUE

THE WIND DROVE the snow with a banshee howl. The streets were deserted as the storm hit New York with brutal force. Only someone insane would be outside now. Only a madman—or someone driven by a force even fiercer than the wind-whipped snow . . .

. . . Such as the figure impossibly perched above the window of a watch repair shop on First Avenue. It was the only shop on the street that was lit. The shadowy figure, half covered in blowing snow, clung upside down to the side of the building, holding on with palms and soles. Slowly it bent lower, and peered through the snowy store window.

Suddenly, bells and whistles began to sound from the store's interior. The startled figure looking in almost fell from his perch. The two men inside the shop jumped. The man in the dark, ankle-length coat screamed and turned around. Now the pistol he held in his hand could be seen.

"What's going on?" the man yelled, panic in his voice.

The old shop owner put his hands up quickly, trying to calm down the thief. "It's midnight," he said. "The clocks are striking twelve. That's all."

The thief snarled and swung the gun back, pointing it at the old man's head. "Cash!" he said, his voice filled with menace. "Open the register. Now!"

The jeweler's hands trembled as he pushed the keys to open the register. But the drawer didn't spring open on the first try.

"What's the matter, gramps?" the gunman said. "You aren't scared, are you?" He gestured with the pistol, a little side-to-side motion. "Hurry it up, and you won't have a thing to worry about."

With a sudden gesture, he smashed the butt of the pistol down on the glass case in front of the register. Shards flew. The jeweler jumped at the sound, and his trembling increased.

Without taking his eyes from the older man, the robber reached into the case. "I need a new watch," he said. After a quick glance, he

The shadowy figure, half-covered in blowing snow, clung upside down to the side of the building . . .

picked out the most expensive one. "This will do."

He put it on his wrist and motioned again with the weapon. "I'm still waiting for my money, gramps. Snap it up. If I'm not out of here by 12:05, you're a dead man!"

An eerie echo of the storm above howled through the tunnels beneath New York's streets. An empty subway train screeched to a stop at the Rector Street station, and pulled out moments later, still empty. But the station was not quite deserted. The uptown side of the platform held two figures.

"Your watch and your wallet," said the smaller of the two men. He held a wicked-looking hunting knife. As he twisted it slowly before the other man's face, light shimmered along its ten-inch blade. "I'm not kidding, man. I'll cut you."

The taller man pulled off his watch and held it out. His hand was trembling.

"A Timex? You're kidding me. Now your wallet!"

In the pipes high overhead, a shadow moved. Neither of the two men below noticed, too intent on each other. Had they looked, they might have seen the large, black-clad figure. It was a massive creature, all in black, except for a white spider design on his chest and back. It had white eye-patches, and large, pointed teeth. Beneath its too-wide grin a foot-long tongue moved like a snake.

The creature was drooling.

In the shop on First Avenue, the robber scooped up the green bills the old man had hastily pulled from the cash register's drawer. "That's all?" he asked. "You're kidding, right? *Where*'s the rest of it?"

"Please," the jeweler said. "It was a slow day. Not many customers. The weather. . . ."

The robber raised his hand—the one with the pistol. "Good night, gramps." His finger tightened on the trigger . . .

. . . Just as a sticky line of white flew from the direction of the door. It hit with a *wap!* and wrapped around the pistol. A split-second later the blue-steel weapon came away from the thief's grip. It flew across the shop and clattered to a stop in the front corner of the store.

The robber yelped as much in fear as in pain. He turned to the door, where he saw an impossible sight. A human figure hung upside down from the doorway, dressed in red and blue, with the black tracing of a spider web over head and shoulders.

"Hi!" the costumed figure said in a cheery voice. "Mind if I drop in?"

He twisted down from the door frame, rolled, and sprang to his feet all in one fluid movement. Then, without pausing, he leapt to an upper corner, where he crouched, impossibly defying gravity.

"Spider-Man!" the store owner cried. "Boy, am I glad to see *you*!"

The robber gave a shout and dashed for the door. Before he'd taken a step, Spider-Man moved. A line of webbing shot from his wrist, curling around the robber's left ankle, tangling and tripping him. The man fell heavily to the floor. A scatter of dollar bills flew from his pocket.

"Aw, don't tell me you want to leave already," Spider-Man said, swinging down from his perch. "We haven't been properly introduced yet," he added, as another line of webbing trussed the robber's hands.

At the Rector Street station, a black shadow plummeted from overhead down to the tracks. It was no more than a blur of motion, that the taller man saw from the corner of his eye.

Yet in that instant, the knife-wielding thief also vanished—grabbed around the ankles by coiling lines of a white substance, and pulled out of sight beneath the platform where the shadow had vanished. The robber was gone, but the knife was still there, spinning on the dirty concrete of the platform. The mugging victim went wide-eyed. Surprised and confused, he slowly lowered his hands.

A moment later, from under the platform, came a blood-curdling cry of fear and pain. It echoed loudly through the empty tunnel and then—suddenly—ended.

A loud pounding on the door brought the desk sergeant at the Third Precinct to his feet. The police officer walked rapidly to the door and jerked it open.

On the icy steps out front he saw a human-shaped bundle, wrapped in a grayish-white, ropy substance. A man's face, eyes wide with fear, was exposed at one end of the bundle.

A voice above the sergeant's head caused him to look up. "Caught him in the act. An armed robbery over at First Avenue Watch Repair," said the costume character. He was attached to the sheer wall by his palms and soles, looking down from that position into the sergeant's face. "The proprietor will be along in a moment to make a statement."

"You can make a statement yourself," the sergeant said. He knew who this fellow was: Spider-Man.

"Sorry, got to go. Previous engagement," the wall-crawling super hero said. With that he flipped up a wrist, flicked a line of webbing to a higher wall across the street, and swung rapidly out of sight.

Beneath the streets the air smelled of hot oil and cold iron. The man on the Rector Street platform stood alone, looking down at the abandoned knife. A shadow appeared before him. He knew who *this* creature was: he'd seen the newspaper photos, heard the stories of blood and death. He fell to his knees.

"Venom," he said, his voice wavering. "Please don't kill me."

"You have nothing to fear from us," the huge figure said. It's tongue waggled and slime dripped from it fangs. "So long as you remain innocent."

The costumed super-villain bent suddenly and placed the man's stolen watch back into his hand.

"We do not harm the innocent. See that you remain so. Else we will be forced to find you and eat your spleen."

The man looked down at the cheap watch in his hand. Was that a tiny drop of blood on the crystal?

When he looked up again, Venom was gone.

CHAPTER 1

THE WINTER STORM howled across the city. Snowflakes were falling thick and fast when Spider-Man got to the steps of city hall.

The view of the nearby Brooklyn Bridge was almost lost in the wall of flying white flakes.

Spidey wasn't late—the news reporters were still getting ready with their microphones and videocameras—but he could tell that he'd cut it close. The mayor's speech was scheduled for 12:15, and it was just a few minutes past noon.

Not all the looks he got were friendly ones as he swung down from the building on the corner. Johnny Storm, the Human Torch, gave Spidey a grin and a wave, and so did one or two other people in the crowd. But J. Jonah Jameson, publisher of the *Daily Bugle*, only glared at him. Jameson didn't like Spider-Man—any news story that involved the web-slinging super hero was guaranteed to make the publisher bad-tempered for at least a week. Jameson was most unhappy about sharing the spotlight with Spider-Man during the First Annual Manhattan Civic Pride Awards ceremony.

Spidey smiled beneath his mask. He could think of one good thing about having an outdoor ceremony on a day like this. Most of the spectators would blame Jameson's angry scowl on the rotten weather rather than Spider-Man's presence. A raw, cold wind blew around the city hall steps.

Only a few people had gathered to watch the awards. Everybody else in the city would see the event at home on the evening news. That was probably why the Mayor hadn't changed his plans for the ceremony when the weather turned nasty. He liked the way he looked on TV with city hall behind him and a bunch of Manhattan's most famous citizens standing around to cover him with reflected glory.

"If you ask me," the Torch said quietly to Spider-Man, "the mayor ought to have postponed the ceremony. I'm not cold, but some of those reporters out there look like they're already frozen."

"That's because they've been standing here longer than anybody else," Spider-Man said. He was glad that, for once, he wasn't among those shivering reporters. The red and blue costume that hid his identity as Peter Parker also protected his face and ears and fingers from the cold, with no gaps that might let in the wind and the snow. "Reporters always show up early. Just in case something important happens before the ceremony even gets started."

"You really think that's likely?"

"No," said Spider-Man. "But if space aliens kidnapped the mayor on his way to the microphone, and the reporters weren't there to cover it, they'd all be in a lot of trouble."

Over at the speaker's platform, the mayor glanced one more time at his notes and began to speak.

"Ladies and gentlemen—"

A squeal of feedback from the speakers made Spidey wince. The mayor adjusted the microphone and tried again.

"Ladies and gentlemen, welcome to the first annual Manhattan Civic Pride Awards Ceremony.

"These awards honor people who have made a difference in this city—people whose hard work and civic spirit gives us all an example to follow—"

Spider-Man already knew what the awards were for. In his other career as Peter Parker, freelance news photographer, he'd heard more than enough of the mayor's speeches. He quit listening, and watched the quickly freezing guests at the ceremony instead.

Johnny Storm—the Human Torch—was standing in for the Fantastic Four. The fair-haired young man belonged to one of the city's best-known and most respected super hero teams, and this wasn't the first time he'd represented the group in public. The video reporters loved him: he had the sort of good looks that would have done a television newsman proud, and the red flame of his super power made him an impressive sight whenever the team went into action.

"—individuals and institutions," the mayor was saying. "They have taken direct and positive steps toward solving the city's problems—"

J. Jonah Jameson's frown grew even deeper. Spider-Man could feel the publisher's dislike for him, even at a distance. It wasn't exactly a threat, not something to set off the tingling awareness of danger that was his spider-sense. But it was an unpleasant sensation just the same. Jameson's bad mood drew the attention of the Torch as well.

"What's eating at him?" the Torch asked under his breath.

Spider-Man shrugged. "I don't think he likes my face."

"Nobody's ever *seen* your face. How would J. Jonah Jameson know whether he liked it or not?"

Spidey smiled and said, "He can tell without looking that if he ever did see my face, he wouldn't like it. Meanwhile, having me around while he hobnobs with the mayor is souring his stomach real bad."

The mayor turned to a new page of his notes, then looked over at one of his aides. The aide brought out a sturdy presentation box. The mayor removed the lid and took out a polished wooden plaque with an engraved brass plate.

"In giving out the first Civic Pride Awards," the mayor said, "the city and the mayor's office—and the Civic Pride Foundation—all felt that we should recognize a group that has done a great deal to protect our city from powerful outside threats. The members of the Fantastic Four—"

"That's your cue," Spidey whispered to Torch. "Don't forget to smile for the cameras."

Johnny Storm stepped up to shake the mayor's hand and accept the plaque.

"We're honored that you think so well of us," Johnny said.

The wind took his words and snatched at them, making his acceptance speech hard to understand in spite of the sound system that had been set up for the occasion. One gust of cold air caught at the sheets of green tissue in the box that had held the plaque. Unweighted, the paper blew away like oversized leaves, flapping and swirling through the falling snowflakes.

Cradling the plaque in one arm, the Torch rejoined Spider-Man. "Your turn next, I think," he said.

He was right.

"—the super hero who recently put a stop to the criminal activities of those predatory super-villains Dr. Octopus, Mysterio, the Hobgoblin, the Shocker, the Vulture, and the Chameleon," the mayor was saying. "Nor have we heard new reports of Venom's outrages. I can't help feeling that this super hero has helped keep that menace at bay, too. The credit belongs to that daring web-slinger —"

Spider-Man could see J. Jonah Jameson's face getting purpler with every complimentary phrase. He hoped that the *Bugle*'s publisher didn't explode from the effort of containing his irritation.

"—Spider-Man!" the mayor finished.

The handful of spectators clapped politely. They were now a soggy bunch, with little drifts of white snow collecting on their collars and their hat brims. Spidey wondered why any of them had bothered to come in the first place. It wasn't his business, he reminded himself as he went up to shake the mayor's hand.

There wasn't any plaque this time. Spidey didn't know whether it was because there was only one of him, instead of a whole team, or because nobody at the Civic Pride Foundation could figure out where Spider-Man would be hanging up a plaque if he got one.

Being anonymous has its little drawbacks, Spidey thought. But it's safer. At least I get to live a sort of normal life when I'm out of costume.

Out loud he said, "Thank you, one and all. Taking care of troublemakers like the Hobgoblin is my pleasure, Your Honor."

He saw Jameson frowning at him again as he stepped back to stand beside the Torch.

"Troublemakers, hah!" the publisher grumbled, not quite loud enough for the microphones to pick it up. "It takes one to know one."

Jameson didn't say anything more. The mayor was already moving into the next part of his speech, and in only a short while the television news cameras would all be turned to the publisher of the *Daily Bugle*.

"—as powerful a force for good," the mayor was saying, "as any super hero, or any team of super heroes—"

Jonah isn't likely to take that as a compliment, Spider-Man thought. As far as Jameson was concerned, a properly run newspaper did more good than all the super heroes in Manhattan put together. He'd certainly said so often enough, over the years, and loudly, too.

"—a fearless and undaunted voice against crime and corruption—"

The mayor was on a roll, Spidey thought, heaping more praise on the *Bugle* than he'd given to the Fantastic Four and Spider-Man put together. Not surprising. The people at the *Daily Bugle* were ordinary men and women—well, *most* of them were ordinary—and the mayor probably felt a lot more wholehearted admiration for them than he did for Spider-Man and the Human Torch.

Sometimes super heroes got a kind of nervous gratitude, Spidey knew, rather than true respect. All too often the thanks he got had a feeling of: "Thank you for everything, especially for not hurting anybody or breaking too many windows while you were busy fighting the forces of evil."

The mayor was still talking. "Most recently, the *Daily Bugle* has tackled the question of crime and homelessness in our city's subways, working to raise public and police awareness of a growing problem. . . ."

The wind had picked up since the awards ceremony began. A sudden gust caught at the mayor's notes and tried to snatch them out of his hands. The mayor gripped the sheets of paper firmly and continued.

"When it comes to dealing with our city's problems, too many people claim that nothing anybody can do will bring results. Just looking at the *Bugle*'s record proves that these nay-sayers are dead wrong. Since the paper began its public-awareness campaign, subway crime has fallen steeply all over Manhattan. Once again an ordinary citizen can ride the IRT at midnight without taking his life in his hands."

J. Jonah Jameson looked pleased to hear the *Bugle* praised, especially in front of the paper's radio and television rivals. But the Torch muttered to Spider-Man, "The mayor needs a lesson in logic, I think."

Spidey nodded. As a physics student at Empire State University, he'd learned a long time ago that just because Event One happened first and Event Two happened later, that didn't mean that the first event had anything to do with causing the second one. The decrease in subway crime could have been brought about by almost anything, from the newspaper campaign to a change in the weather.

"You're right," he said to the Torch. "But we can't say for sure that the people at Jameson's paper *didn't* help make things better, either. At least they tried."

The *Bugle* did get a plaque, a large and impressive one. J. Jonah Jameson accepted it on behalf of the newspaper. The Mayor turned to the next page of his speech.

"Finally," the mayor said, "it's time to thank two people who were out on the front line of the *Bugle*'s campaign. I'm talking about the reporter and the photographer whose series of articles on the violence and poverty underneath our streets did so much to focus the issue in the public eye."

J. Jonah Jameson was frowning again in spite of the fact that it was two of his own people who were being honored. Spider-Man knew what was upsetting Jameson this time. It wasn't so much sharing credit. It was the fact that he had to share it with Peter Parker.

"It gives me great pleasure," the mayor said, "to present the Civic Pride Foundation's first annual Special Prize for News Reporting in the Public Interest to Ben Urich and to Peter Parker—the writer and the photographer for the feature series, 'Life and Death Beneath Manhattan.' It further pleases me to announce that a gift from an anonymous donor has allowed the foundation to accompany the prize with a substantial monetary award, to be divided between the writer and the photographer."

The reporter, Ben Urich, a thin man with heavy-framed glasses, came forward to accept his share of the prize. He looked pleased in spite of the fact that the steadily falling snow had marked out the creases of his dark overcoat with lines of white. His nose and ears were red from the wind, but he was smiling as he took the envelope from the mayor's hand. The check inside the envelope, Spider-Man had reason to know, would be a sizable one, enough to make any working reporter happy.

"Mr. Urich's words provided the city with a call to action," the Mayor said. "And the dramatic pictures that accompanied his articles showed us all just how much that action was needed. As much as anybody else we're honoring today, photographer Peter Parker deserves credit for helping clean up the city's subways. Mr. Parker?"

For a moment, nobody came forward. Then J. Jonah Jameson, his frown deeper than ever, stepped up to take the envelope.

"Mr. Parker couldn't be here today," Jameson told the Mayor. "Personal reasons, he said."

Spider-Man heard the growl in Jameson's voice and winced. Peter Parker would hear all about unreliable—and ungrateful!—freelancers later this evening when he dropped by the *Bugle*'s offices to pick up the prize money. But it couldn't be helped. Any time Spider-Man and Peter Parker had invitations to the same party, only one of them was going to show up.

CHAPTER
—2—

"ONE HUNDRED TWELVE . . . one hundred thirteen . . . one hundred fourteen," the man huffed. The arched walls of gray cement echoed the sounds of his explosive breathing. He pushed the huge barbells directly up from his chest, then lowered them again with each number counted aloud. He was lying on a bench, pressing the bar high.

"One hundred fifteen."

Eddie Brock paused, with the barbells held above him, his arms braced. Then he lowered the barbells slowly into their rack and relaxed.

The burn was back in his muscles, and it felt good. Sweat was streaming from his forehead, and that felt good too. Eddie had worked hard to make himself as strong as it was possible for a normal man to become. And with a regular set of exercises, repeated daily, he kept himself in top condition.

Behind the weight bench, a voice was droning. Eddie wasn't paying much attention. He'd tapped into the cables running beneath New York City in order to provide electricity for his underground home, and he'd allowed himself the luxury of bringing in a cable TV feed while he was at it. The voices kept the loneliness away, and the television news provided a line on what was happening in the world above.

Eddie sat up after a few more deep breaths, and reached for a towel.

"Live from city hall!" came the voice of the television announcer, as Eddie mopped the sweat off his face and slung the towel around his neck. He didn't envy the TV people, standing out in the cold and wind. He'd done his time as a reporter, going out in all kinds of weather, talking to all kinds of people, putting together the facts to write the stories, doing the research. That had been fun in its own way, and he was getting back into it slowly.

Still sitting on the bench, he slid his hands under the bar and gripped it. He raised the weights overhead, then lowered them to his shoulders. The towel around his neck padded the hard metal shaft of the bar.

"One . . . two . . . ."

Counting slowly, Eddie began a series of

trunk twists. The television came into view each time he swung all the way to his right, then vanished as he swung to the left. The heavy weight pressing down on his shoulders forced him to keep a steady, unhurried pace.

" . . . twenty-three . . . twenty-four . . . twenty-five. . . ."

Something about one of those figures on the city hall steps, glimpsed out of the corner of his eye, reminded Eddie of someone.

"Twenty-six . . . "He turned again, continuing his exercise set, not breaking the rhythm.

"Twenty-seven . . . " He turned back.

Yes, there, in the little group to the mayor's left.

". . . Twenty-eight . . ."

Spider-Man.

Eddie could feel his shoulders going tense, tenser than the weight of the barbells could account for.

Spider-Man! What was that little punk doing up there? Brock felt a surge of rage. Even after all this time. He fought it down.

A black film rippled over Brock's chest.

"Steady, steady," he said, holding on to his reason. He forced himself to continue the mechanical motions of his exercise set. "Twenty-nine."

The black film retreated.

Eddie Brock had once been an ace reporter

for the *Daily Globe*. He'd been near the top of his profession, and rising fast. Then he got an exclusive, an interview with the serial killer called the Sin-Eater. The story was printed in the *Globe* only hours before Spider-Man caught the real Sin-Eater. And Eddie Brock's world came crashing down. His self-image shattered when the hoax was revealed. He blamed not himself but Spider-Man for the disgrace . . . for what he considered his loss of innocence.

"Thirty."

The mayor was still talking. Eddie could make out some of what he was saying.

"—direct and positive steps—"

"Right," Eddie said, replacing the barbells on their stand, pausing between exercise sets. "The only one taking direct and positive steps is *us*."

Again the black film rippled across his chest.

Eddie Brock had a constant companion: an alien symbiote. It could cover him in an instant with an impermeable membrane. It adjusted to his movements, it heightened his abilities. And it shared his rage.

Just as Eddie Brock felt that Spider-Man had destroyed him, the alien symbiote felt betrayed by Spider-Man. Of course, if Spider-Man had known the strange costume was alive, he never would have taken it back home in the first place. He had gotten the costume on an alien world, during an all-out battle of the forces of good against evil known as the Secret War. His original costume had been ripped to shreds during the battle, but Spidey had found a mysterious machine that had created a new, sleek, black-and-white outfit for him.

Back on Earth, Spider-Man found that the new costume seemed to respond to his every thought. It would shrink back from his mouth when he wanted to drink. It was capable of changing into ordinary looking street clothes, so that Spidey could wear his costume all the time. When he needed to go into action, the street clothes would magically morph back into his costume.

But when he started having nightmares about it, he took it to Reed Richards for analysis. Richards, leader of the Fantastic Four and one of the world's foremost scientists, had shocking news: the costume was alive! More than that, it was a symbiote—a living creature that needed to bond with a host in order to survive.

Spider-Man tried several ways to induce the creature to leave him. But after he had learned that the symbiote wanted to join with him forever, he'd used sound waves to destroy the creature.

At least, he'd *thought* that he had destroyed it.

The symbiote was driven away by the sonic blasts, but it did not die. It clung to its alien half-life until it found someone who shared its hatred of Spider-Man. Found him, and bonded with him. Became one with Eddie Brock. Together they became Venom—a creature with razor-sharp fangs, a lashing tongue, and a hunger for the blood and spleens of malefactors.

Venom defined who or what a malefactor was, and to Venom, Spider-Man was the ultimate evil.

"Calmly," Eddie said. Reassuring himself. Steadying himself.

He picked up a pair of dumbbells, massive weights that most ordinary men would have had trouble lifting with both hands, and commenced a set of biceps curls. He turned his back on the television, letting it run on as a droning sound behind him. Against the opposite wall was a desk, where a stack of correspondence—he had a post-office box in Brooklyn, rented under a false name—waited for his attention.

No one would ever buy a story from Eddie Brock again, not after the Sin-Eater fiasco, but *Edward Badger* was finally starting to get assignments. Not from the supermarket tabloids, either, but from the slick magazines. His other career was coming back. He wouldn't let anyone take that away from him. Not again.

Muscles pumped as Eddie's arms flexed and straightened like parts of a living machine. The lights on the ceiling shook as a subway train passed by overhead.

Brock's underground home was a section of subway tunnel abandoned and sealed off for more than thirty years. The gray walls of the tunnels were arched to the center of the ceiling. Everything he had here, like the electricity to power the lights and the cable for the television set, had been informally borrowed from the city by means of late-night wire splicing and pipefitting.

He put more effort into the exercise. The more you put in, the more you get out, he reminded himself. That was true for everything, from exercise to life in general.

Brock had made a point of giving, in his own way, to the underground world where he now lived. Thanks to Venom, the subways of New York were now safer, no matter what the hour. Those who preyed on the innocent had by their free choice already forfeited their lives, the way Venom saw it.

"They can't take that away from me," he muttered. "We're doing more good than the lot of them combined."

Doing good crudely, true—but doing it effectively. Venom felt strongly that what counted in the long run was results. Not how they were achieved.

"Results . . . if I have enough breath to talk to myself, I'm not working hard enough."

He redoubled his efforts with the hand weights, changing from bicep curls to tricep extensions. But under the repetitive motions of the exercise, his mind ran on unchecked.

His eyes strayed back to the TV screen. Spider-Man was on the platform beside the mayor. *Spider-Man.* All Spider-Man had done to become a super hero was get bitten by a radioactive spider. Eddie had made himself strong through hard work. Spider-Man had it handed to him, Eddie thought bitterly.

The mayor's voice broke into his reverie. "—predatory super-villains Dr. Octopus, Mysterio, the Hobgoblin—"

The Sinister Six: Spider-Man's foes. Eddie knew that the web-slinger had captured the lot of them recently.

Here comes some more garbage about the man who has ruined my life, Brock thought. Then he heard another name, one that he knew as well as his own.

"—reports of Venom's outrages—"

With a snarl of anger Brock threw the weights away from him. They crashed into the far wall, gouging chips from the cement. The black membrane of his living costume spread across Eddie's body like a splash of ink, flowing swiftly across him.

Brock and the symbiote were one, and Venom's foot-long tongue lashed in front of their eyes.

"Outrages!" Venom roared.

They leaned forward to fix their blank white eyes on the TV screen. Their hands grasped the edge of Eddie Brock's weight bench, and their fingers crumbled the solid wood into splinters. "Our 'outrages' have made this city a better place!"

Then Venom froze. "And that fool gives 'credit' to Spider-Man for the fact that we choose—we *choose*!—to remain out of sight and do our work in private."

Venom's alien eyes watched, expressionless, as Spider-Man stepped forward to accept the award.

"And he takes the credit he *knows* he does not deserve. We did not suspect that even Spider-Man could sink this low. Perhaps, perhaps we should visit the mayor and explain. Perhaps he will have an award for *us*."

Venom cocked a wrist and shot a line of webbing into an access hole on the ceiling of Eddie Brock's underground home. In an instant they were gone, up into the maze of publicly known tunnels, then out a moment later into the freezing air of the city. Venom threw a web line to a high point on a building and swung away into the stormy afternoon.

High between the buildings, the wind whipped snowflakes with blizzard force. Had Eddie's human skin not been protected by its symbiotic covering, the icy blast would have stung him to the bone. As it was, the black and white of Venom's costume provided excellent camouflage. They made their way rapidly among the concrete towers of midtown, heading to city hall between Broadway and Chambers Street in the southern part of Manhattan.

They arrived minutes later. Venom clung to the high side of a building on the other side of the square. The human-alien creature waited, listening. The mayor's voice was amplified to carry over the wind.

"—Peter Parker deserves the credit for cleaning up the city subways—"

"Peter Parker!"

Venom's shout of astonishment and rage echoed from the buildings around the square.

"We know who you are, Peter Parker," Venom said, more quietly.

It was true. Eddie Brock, and Venom, knew more about Spider-Man than almost anyone alive. They knew where he lived, they knew where he worked.

The black membrane of his living costume spread across Eddie's body like a splash of ink flowing swiftly across him.

They knew his secret identity.

We are getting better able to control ourselves, Venom thought. Another time they would have leapt down in front of everyone to rip out Spider-Man's spleen. Now the rage was cold in Venom's gut, colder than the lashing snow.

"We will destroy you," Venom whispered. "You stole our lives, and now you take credit for our deeds. We will destroy you in both of your guises. Spider-Man *and* Peter Parker will know what it is to steal from Venom!"

CHAPTER 3

THE MAYOR LEFT the microphones and headed back inside city hall, flanked by a group of city officials.

"I guess that's it, Spidey," the Torch said. "Show's over."

The two of them were the only costumed characters present. The others who had been honored at the mayor's ceremony were passing wide around them, as if whatever they had might be catching.

Most ordinary folks respected and trusted super heroes like the Fantastic Four and Captain America, Spider-Man thought. But my reputation isn't quite so good, in spite of the mayor's glowing words. Not everyone in the city was as down on Spider-Man as J. Jonah Jameson. But the publisher of the *Daily Bugle* wasn't alone in his opinions.

A fierce gust of icy wind sent a white blur of snow swirling down the street.

"Looks like it's time to go," Spider-Man said. "Where are you heading? Back to Four Freedoms Plaza?"

The Torch nodded. "That's right. I'm holding down the office. The rest of the team is off in Turkestan dealing with a volcano. I have to go back and check for messages on the answering machine."

"How did you get so lucky?"

"It was my turn," the Torch said. "Someone had to stay behind and do a few repairs at headquarters. Reed left me with a shopping list—electronic stuff, mostly. I'm going to pick it up on the way back to headquarters. Want to come along?"

"Sure," Spider-Man said.

He wouldn't mind a few more minutes chatting with his old friend, he thought, and he could always do some window-shopping of his own. He had a serious love for gadgetry, as well as a serious lack of the cash to buy it. With the prize money coming, he could return to the store later as Peter Parker and pick up a few things.

"Come on, then," Johnny Storm said. "Let's give the folks on the street a show." He checked around, saw no close bystanders, and shouted "Flame on!"

The Torch rose in the air like a streak of crimson fire against the low-hanging clouds. Spider-Man shot a line of webbing to the top of a building across the plaza, and hurried to catch up. Spider-Man didn't realize it, but the place he'd chosen to attach his web for his next swing wasn't far from where Venom had crouched not many minutes before.

Crime is down, Spider-Man said to himself. Nobody's seen Venom around in months. And my spider sense isn't tingling. He launched another sticky strand to the top corner of a building ahead and swung farther uptown.

So why, he wondered, am I feeling worried?

He couldn't think of a reason. Part of Peter's award check would help out with the household finances, and the publicity from that series of photos might let him ask for a little extra for his other shots as well.

As a photographer, Spidey reminded himself, I'm not just Peter Parker any more. I'm The Award-Winning Peter Parker. *Life is good.*

"Where to?" Spider-Man said to his companion. He had to shout to make himself heard over the wind that moaned among the high buildings.

A sudden gust caught Spider-Man and buffeted him, hard, just as he finished his question. The crosswinds today were affecting his progress around the city. He had to watch his web placement a lot more carefully than usual. But so far the weather didn't seem to be affecting the Torch at all.

"Sam's Radio and Electronics," Johnny called back. "We have an account. Right down—*there.*"

"I see it!"

Spider-Man performed a graceful curl and tuck in the air. He landed on the wall beside the electronics store, using his spider power to cling to the rough brick with his hands and feet. He leapt to the sidewalk just as the Torch shouted "Flame off!" and touched down to the pavement.

The Torch became once again a cheerful, blond-haired young man dressed in the uniform of the Fantastic Four. Spider-Man followed Johnny Storm into the store.

High banks of shelves filled with electronics lined the walls. A ladder on rails would allow a clerk to check the bins that were too high to reach from the floor. The rosin smell of silvery solder hung in the air. Behind a counter, a middle-aged woman sat at a workbench, a tripod-mounted magnifying glass between her and her work. To Spider-Man it seemed that she was mounting a relay into some kind of robotic arm.

"Hiya, Sam," Johnny called.

"Hey, Johnny," the woman said. She made a sketchy salute in the air with the tiny screwdriver she held in her right hand before turning back to the robotic arm. "What can I do for you—and your friend—today?"

"Spidey's just looking around. I need parts for the sonic gun," Johnny said. "And a few other things. We're going to get the gravometric wave detector working reliably one of these days, as soon as the feedback problem's licked. Have any capacitors in the picofarad range with built-in heat sinks?"

"Bins over there. Help yourself looking around."

Meanwhile, Spider-Man had wandered over to the audio/video section. A new sound system for the apartment would be nice, he thought. Both Peter Parker and his wife, Mary Jane, liked music, but their current system left something—well, quite a bit, really—to be desired. Near the audio components, a wall of TV sets all tuned to the same station showed a soap opera in progress. A young doctor had just had his advances rebuffed by a young nurse, in a plot thread that had probably been going on for months and still had months to go.

"Hey, mister, are you Spider-Man?"

Spidey looked down.

A kid about ten years old, bundled up in

mittens, a too-long woolen scarf, and a parka, looked back up at him. "If you're really Spider-Man, can I have your autograph?"

"Sure," Spidey said. "Do you have something for me to sign?"

"You mean you don't have any cards or anything?"

"Matter of fact, no," Spidey replied. "Ah, while you're at it, do you have a pen?"

"Gee, don't you carry a pen?"

"No," Spider-Man said. "I suppose I ought to, though."

Another, older kid came up behind the autograph seeker. "Hey, Billy—forget him. Johnny Storm is here!"

"Wow!" the younger kid exclaimed. He turned away without looking back at Spider-Man. "I *told* you I saw the Torch landing out there! Let's go get *his* autograph!"

Good thing I'm not in this business to feed my ego, Spider-Man thought. He turned back to the shelves. As he turned, a line of type scrolled across the bottom of each of the television sets, repeated a dozen times in slightly different sizes depending on the measurement of the TV screens.

"SEVERE WINTER STORM WARNING," the message read. "AVOID UNNECESSARY TRAVEL. SNOW EMERGENCY PARKING RULES ARE IN EFFECT."

Nothing in that to bother a friendly neighborhood Spider-Man, Spidey thought. Maybe it'll keep a few criminals home and I can have an easy night.

Then the TV cut away from the soap opera to the station's "News As It Happens" logo. The logo faded to a live announcer sitting behind a desk, looking serious.

"This just in," the announcer said, while behind him the video showed Spider-Man standing on the steps of city hall. "Minutes after receiving a civic award from the mayor, Spider-Man apparently robbed the Seaforth Trust bank branch on West Forty-Third Street. Witnesses report that a costumed villain dressed in red and blue entered the bank, demanded cash, then escaped by swinging away on web-lines he shot from his hands."

The Torch had come over to stand beside Spidey while the news bulletin was in progress. "Don't worry," Johnny Storm said. "You have an alibi. Two witnesses, me and Sam—four if you count the kids."

Now the news report was showing person-in-the-street interviews from the robbery scene. Most of the people were saying that the perpetrator must have been an impostor: "Spider-Man is one of the good guys, isn't he?" said an eyewitness. But one man, a burly fellow in a business suit, commented, "Spider-

Man? I've always wondered about him. Nobody's seen his face, no one knows where he lives. It doesn't surprise me that he's started robbing banks."

"So much for the admiration of the crowd," Spidey said. The announcer promised details at six, then cut away to a commercial.

"Come on," Johnny said. "No one can possibly believe that you've turned into a bank robber."

"It's nice of you to say so," Spider-Man said. His vision of surprising MJ with a new sound system had been driven out of his mind by the news. "But some people obviously do believe it. I bet I can figure out the headline the *Bugle* is going to run on the late edition: SPIDER-MAN ROBS BANK. And people who don't believe it the first time might believe it the second, or the third. If this guy keeps robbing banks dressed like me, there are going to be times when I don't have reliable witnesses who can testify that they saw me in a different part of town."

"Okay. We'll just have to catch this guy before then."

"If that 'we' was an offer of help, then I accept," Spidey said gratefully.

He tried to sound upbeat and cheerful, but he knew how fickle public opinion could be.

Reputation is a fragile thing, and Spider-Man's reputation had always been a little bit shaky.

At the same time, questions were forming at the back of his mind: Who could be doing this? Who hated him? And who—out of all his enemies—could swing on a web?

When he thought about it that way, the answer came to him almost at once.

Venom.

The alien symbiote-suit could look like any article of clothing, including its normal black with a white spider, or Spider-Man's own distinctive red and blue. For that matter, the man who had been interviewed, the big, heavy-set guy in the business suit, had looked somehow familiar.

Then Spider-Man knew. The businessman had been Eddie Brock. The war was starting again.

Spider-Man didn't have a clue as to what had triggered Venom this time. Just the fact that Spider-Man was still alive might have been enough to set Venom off in a homicidal rage.

"Johnny, I'll see you later," he said. "I have a few things to do first. This is going to be a long night."

CHAPTER
—4—

SPIDER-MAN HURRIED out of Sam's Electronics. He leapt up as he passed the threshold, grabbed the lintel, and twisted himself up to the wall above, just in time to miss being splashed by a wave of slush tossed up by a passing bus. The streets were filled with a foot of dirty brown slush. The sidewalks were turning into churned white paths. The wind was rising, and the snow was falling faster.

Spider-Man looked for a place to shoot his web-line. It was hard to see through the snow. He found a spot on the high corner of a building opposite and shot a web-line. The wind made aiming difficult. When the web made contact, he let go of the wall and swung out over the street. Before he'd gotten halfway across, he was shooting another web to the top of a second building, guiding his course farther uptown to where he had left the backpack that held his civilian clothes.

He found the pack as he'd left it, tied up with webbing and protected from the weather by an overhanging balcony. He took the package and swung quickly down into an alley.

Moments later he had changed and emerged from the alley looking like a typical New Yorker, except for the camera hung around his neck.

Peter Parker needed to get over to the *Daily Bugle* offices to pick up that prize money, then make it to his bank to deposit the check. If he hurried, he could get the check in before the bank closed for the day.

He hadn't realized how bad the weather was getting. The snow on the sidewalks was higher than the tops of his shoes, and his short jacket wasn't anywhere near warm enough. Without the protection of his costume the wind-driven ice crystals burned the skin of his face and hands.

Other than by web-slinging, the fastest way to reach the *Bugle* offices was by subway. That method also had the advantage of keeping him out of the weather. Peter found a subway entrance and went down.

The streets above had become almost deserted as the storm grew worse, and now Peter saw that most of the foot traffic had gone into the tunnels instead. At least it wasn't too cold down here, he thought, even if water was dripping from the ceiling in one place and more slush was being tracked down the stairs all the time. The subway platform was wet with half-melted snow.

Peter slipped a token into the slot on the turnstile and walked through to join the others who waited on the uptown side of the platform.

And here came the train. The doors opened, and Peter—along with scores of others—pushed on board while others pushed off. Peter was able to squeeze into a place holding onto a pole near the center of the car.

The subway train started with a lurch. Peter swayed with the motion of the car and watched the lights that flickered by outside the windows. When no lights shone in the tunnels outside, the windows were like mirrors, reflecting the interior of the car. And in the reflection he saw a face. A face covered all in midnight black, with huge blank eyes and white fangs in a gaping mouth that stretched from one side of the face to the other.

Venom.

Peter tried to spin around and confront his foe.

But before he could turn, he was caught in the crush when the train stopped abruptly. People were thrown forward.

Maybe someone pulled the emergency brake, Peter thought. Maybe it's Venom, throwing a pseudopod from its body to do the job at a distance.

The lights in the car flashed off. Voices rose, a baby cried, and passengers began pushing each other in the dark. Then a window shattered, one of the vandal-proof unbreakable windows of the subway. The lights suddenly came back on, and the car started on its way again—with two passengers fewer.

Peter found himself lying on his back on the cold gritty floor of a subway tunnel, looking up at a grinning, fang-filled mouth an inch away from his nose.

"Venom," Peter said. "How *nice* to see you. To what do I owe the pleasure?"

Peter wasn't in costume. He wasn't ready for this. Being dressed in his street clothes had always meant he was off duty. Villains from his other, crime-fighting life hadn't reached out to attack him when he was just an ordinary photographer and university student.

But that didn't mean that he couldn't or wouldn't fight back now. Unlike Venom, Peter didn't get his super powers from a special suit. His spider senses and powers were part of him. All he'd added were the web canisters that enabled him to swing around town.

Venom lifted Peter up by his jacket. "That

idiot in Gracie Mansion thinks you've put an end to the Venom menace, does he?" Venom snarled. "Before we're done he'll thank us for putting an end to the Spider-Man menace!"

At least that made some kind of sense, Peter thought. Not a lot of sense, but enough for a paranoid lunatic like Venom.

"You're aware that I didn't write the mayor's speech," Peter asked in a pleasant tone. He was stalling for time. As his eyes adjusted to the darkness, he could start to make out the outlines of this section of tunnel. Pipes here, an access tunnel there—closed with a metal grating sealed with a padlock.

"I know you didn't write it," Venom said. His voice was low and dangerous. His grip on the front of Peter's jacket tightened painfully. "But you did decide to walk up and accept the award. You had a chance to stand up and say, 'But Your Honor, I *didn't* end the Venom menace—Venom is the protector of the innocent and Venom is still here.' You had the chance, but you decided to keep silent and take credit for something you didn't deserve."

Peter reached out slowly with his right hand. There. His fingers touched a pipe. With a lunge he grabbed and pulled it free from its brackets. As part of the same movement he swung it down against the back of Venom's head.

"Oooh, that *smarts*!" Venom said with a laugh—but he lost his grip on the front of Peter's jacket. Peter rolled away and sprang up to the ceiling of the tunnel. A rush of air told him a train was coming.

The worst thing about fighting Venom, Peter decided, was that his spider senses were useless. The black symbiote suit had been designed for Spider-Man in the first place, and it didn't produce anything that its intended wearer would interpret as a signal of approaching danger. That worked great as long as Peter was the one wearing the alien, but when someone else—like Eddie Brock—had the symbiote wrapped around his body, that somebody else was also undetectable to spider sense.

Now Peter had to rely on his eyes and ears alone. He hadn't had a lot of experience fighting that way—which left him at a big disadvantage, since all his practice and training had assumed his spider senses would help to watch his back.

The lights of the approaching train reflected from the walls of the tunnel. The roar was deafening, the lights blinding. No vision, no hearing, no spider sense—and at that moment Venom attacked from the rear. He'd used his time wisely to sneak around behind and launch himself at the wall-crawler.

The attack tore Peter from his perch and sent him tumbling onto the tracks in front of the approaching train with no time to leap clear. Peter threw himself down on the tracks, making himself as flat as he could in the space between the rails. The train roared past in a blur of steel only inches over his head.

I can't be here when the train goes, Peter thought. Venom will be waiting. This time let's give *him* the big surprise.

Peter counted the clacking of the wheels passing by to either side. When he got the rhythm and knew where the wheels were, he rolled away toward the side of the tunnel. He came to rest against the concrete of the tunnel wall, with not a whole lot of room between him and the thundering steel of the subway train.

Good enough, Peter thought. He began to crawl up the side of the tunnel until his head peeked above the roof of the train. Just as he thought: there was Venom, waiting to see how many slices his enemy had been chopped into. Venom was looking down at the train, not up across at the wall. Well, that was about to change.

Peter dived forward, curling into a ball as he went. He slapped the top of the subway train with both palms, changing direction and cannonballing right into Venom's face.

The lights of the approaching train reflected from the walls of the tunnel. The roar was deafening, the lights blinding.

"Surprise, big guy!" Peter called out as he knocked Venom from his position on the wall.

The two of them fell heavily onto the top of the passing train, with Peter on the bottom of the pile. He shoved upward with his legs, lifting Venom high enough for a low-hanging beam to catch the super-villain and snatch him away as the train sped on by underneath.

Peter somersaulted backward and leapt down to the tracks behind the rapidly-vanishing train. In the dim light he could find no sign of his foe.

"If I were Venom," he mused aloud, "where would I run to?"

The answer came a second later as a powerful blow caught him in the back of the head and drove him into the tunnel wall.

"Tag—you're it!" Venom shouted.

Peter dropped and rolled, then jumped to the top of the tunnel where a length of cable provided him with a place to grab on and some shadows in which to hide. A moment later he swung out and down, holding on to the cables with his hands, smashing his feet into Venom as the super-villain passed beneath.

The force of the impact sent Venom crashing into the rails twenty feet away. He bounced to his feet, apparently unhurt, then sprang again toward Peter.

What's his game? Peter wondered. There's something really wrong here, and I don't know—

He didn't have time to finish the thought. Venom was on him, a heavy fist crashing into his side and driving the air from his lungs. Peter ducked the next blow, jumped over the one after that, and turned to launch a powerful kick at Venom's face.

"I thought we had some kind of truce," Peter said as the kick connected. "You know—you don't come looking for me and I don't have to suit up and go looking for you?"

"Truce?" Venom snarled. The kick hadn't even fazed him. "With a destroyer of innocents like you? Not likely."

Peter blocked a backhanded swipe from Venom's left hand. "I have a question," he said, counterpunching as he spoke. "You had a chance to kill me on the subway train. Why didn't you?"

"You haven't figured it out?" Venom sounded genuinely surprised. "We're still going to eat your brains," he continued, sweeping Peter's legs from beneath him and throwing himself on Peter as he fell, "but first we're going to destroy you."

"Somehow—" Peter gasped, punching upward before rolling away "—I fail to see the distinction."

He lunged to his right, then dodged left and crashed down with both fists on Venom's broad back.

Venom twisted, grabbed Peter's right arm, and threw him farther down the track. It was all Peter could do to avoid the third rail, where ten thousand volts of the direct current that powered the subway waited to fry any hapless super hero who might touch it.

Peter noticed something. The tunnel was a lot lighter here than it had been where Venom had so rudely removed him from the train. They must be getting near a station. If anybody happened to see Peter Parker fighting Venom—and fighting him in Spider-Man's inimitable wall-crawling, ceiling-sticking style—that person would know what Spider-Man looked like without his mask.

And then it would be goodbye, secret identity.

With no secret identity, Peter Parker could look forward to dozens of lawsuits from the owners of property that had been accidentally damaged in the course of putting away assorted super-villains. He'd probably spend the rest of his life in court—if not in jail—and he'd end up penniless to boot.

"I don't like the way this fight is going," he said. "Let's go the other way for a while."

"No thanks," Venom said. His fist smashed

Peter in the chest, driving him a little closer to the light of the platform. "We like the way it's going just fine."

Peter rolled and then jumped. He didn't have any web canisters strapped to his wrists, not in his street clothes, but he still had his climbing and clinging ability. He crawled quickly to the top of the tunnel, then started off at high speed into the relative safety of the dark.

Venom didn't need web canisters. His webbing was organic, a substance created by the alien suit itself. Peter heard a web-line sizzle though the air and attach itself close by. Then Venom swung up beside him.

"Bet you're wishing you hadn't abandoned your symbiote now," Venom said. "No worries about getting caught without your costume, no worries about leaving your webs at home."

"I'm not a bit sorry," Peter said. He scuttled farther away down the tunnel. "It was trying to bond to me permanently. I had to get rid of it."

Venom punched up at Peter. "Had to. An awful lot of bad things have been done in the name of had to."

Peter dodged, dropped, then jumped back to the opposite wall. Venom had vanished into the darkness once again. Peter continued into the tunnels.

A rush of air and a gleam of headlights along the tracks signaled the coming of another train. Peter jumped to the ceiling and clung there, flattening himself to avoid the oncoming steel and aluminum juggernaut. Then Venom was on him again.

Peter grasped the pipes at the top of the tunnel with both hands and wrapped his legs in a powerful scissor grip around Venom's waist. Then he pushed off with his feet, swinging Venom down, directly in front of the train. He heard the sound of impact as the front of the first car hit Venom and snatched him away.

Peter swung back up, holding tight as the train passed. When it had gone, he dropped lightly to the tracks. No sign of Venom. With the alien suit to protect him from serious damage, he must have been carried away on the front of the train like a very odd hood ornament.

Still, Peter knew this fight wasn't over, not in the larger sense. Venom had as much as said that he had some scheme going that went beyond merely killing his enemy.

"Later's the time to think about that," Peter said to himself. He found a catwalk along the side of the tracks, and jogged back to the previous station.

He climbed up onto the platform, drawing only a few bored glances from the waiting crowd—if a crazy guy wanted to play tag with a subway train, it wasn't any problem of theirs. He paused to take stock of the damage he'd taken during the fight. His face and hands were smeared with dirt, his trousers had a rip down one side, and worst of all, his camera was smashed.

"Just great, something else to replace," he muttered, and walked up the stairway to the street.

In the fear and excitement of his fight with Venom, he'd almost forgotten about the weather outside. Now it hit him—literally—as he came up out of the station. The wind was blowing harder than ever, and the snow on the sidewalks came well up to his shins.

Before he'd gone more than three steps both his shoes were full of icy crystals. The snow melted in his shoes, making his socks clammy, his feet cold and wet. Next time he stashed his street clothes, he thought, he'd have to remember to include a pair of boots. He trudged on, feeling more miserable than he had in quite a while.

"At least there's some money waiting for me at the *Bugle*," he muttered. "Today won't have been a complete waste."

CHAPTER
—5—

TRAFFIC IN THE STREET had almost come to a halt in the drifting snow. Peter trudged the blocks to the *Daily Bugle* feeling wet and miserable, beaten up in mind and body. Only the prospect of the prize check—and maybe an impromptu party in honor of the *Bugle*'s share of the glory—kept him going. At the very least, someone at the office had probably sent out for pizza.

Finally, after a long trek that left him tired, wet, and chilled, Peter turned in at the door to the *Bugle* building. Once he got warm and dry, and put on some snow boots, maybe he could pick up an assignment to do a "New York Faces the Storm" picture story.

He walked through the lobby and went to the elevator. A few minutes later, he was in the City Room. To his surprise, a party wasn't in progress. If anything, the mood in the City Room was chillier than the wind outside.

The *Bugle* was a big paper, and everyone in the City Room seemed to be purposely ignoring Peter as he walked by. Typewriters fell silent as he passed, and he imagined he could hear whispers. Peter grew more puzzled as he went. He knew almost everyone by sight, although he couldn't put a name to all of the freelancers who passed through the building on a semi-regular basis. But someone who knew him well enough to say hello should have been around. A serving of cold shoulder like this was unusual.

Peter headed through Editorial to the glassed-in rear section where his editor, Kate Cushing, had her office. She opened the door and pointed at him before he could get there.

"Right," Kate said. "Parker. You took your own sweet time about getting here. I've been calling all over town trying to track you down." She looked at him critically for a moment. "What happened to you? Have you been sleeping in a gutter? Never mind that. Mr. Jameson wants to talk to you, and I mean right now."

Everyone in the room looked up. This was out of character for Kate. Usually she was kind, if firm, with her freelancers. Now her voice was strained.

At that same moment, another voice made everyone's head swivel around.

"Parker's here, and I want him!"

J. Jonah Jameson's voice was unmistakable. The man himself followed his voice into the room a few seconds later. Jameson was steaming as he waved a sheaf of 8x10 black and white photos in the air.

"Suppose you explain these!" Jameson said. He shoved the photos under Peter's nose. They looked, to Peter, like copies of his prize-winning shots of homeless people and crime in the city's subways. "Do you have anything to say for yourself?"

"Only that I'm totally confused," Peter said. "What's the matter? Those are my pictures, and the *Bugle* just got a prize for running them."

"Not any more, it doesn't!" Jameson said, his voice getting even louder. "Do you know where I've just been?"

Jameson didn't wait for an answer. "I've been on the phone, that's where. And do you know who I've been on the phone with?" Again he didn't wait for an answer. "I've been talking to the Civic Pride Foundation. They're taking back the prize! The *Bugle*'s prize! And do you know why? Because those photos of yours were faked!"

"They're . . . faked?"

"Ha! You admit it!"

"I admit no such thing!" Peter said. He was getting a little hot under the collar himself by now. Getting that story had taken him to some of the worst spots of the city, camera in hand, looking for the perfect shot, the perfect lighting, the right composition. He was proud of the professional quality of the work he'd done—he felt it was some of his best. "Who says those are fakes?"

"Someone went to the Civic Pride Foundation and told them that you'd paid him to dress up like a bum and sit in a doorway. It seems he showed up wearing the same clothes as in this picture. How do you explain that?"

Ben Urich, the reporter, stepped into the room. He was wearing his rumpled trench coat, wet with melting snow. His heavy-framed glasses were steamed up from coming into a warm place from outdoors.

"Okay," he said. "What's going on?"

"Our young Mr. Parker has been making a monkey out of this paper!" Jameson said, turning and yelling directly into Ben's face. "And when the *Globe* finds out, you can bet they'll run the story on page one!"

"Keep calm," Ben replied quietly. He'd been around the paper for a long time, and was used to Jameson's rants. As if following his own advice, he quietly took off his coat and folded it over his arm. When he'd done so, he looked directly back at Jameson.

"I heard about the problem," he said. "I suppose you realize that whoever accused Peter of creating a hoax is accusing *me* of the same thing. I was with Peter the whole time we were working on that story. Are you accusing me of lying?"

"Somebody's lying, that's for sure!"

"No reason to assume that it's Peter," Ben said in an even tone. He took off his glasses and methodically cleaned them before putting them back on. "He's done excellent work in the past, and you've got to admit that he's brought back pictures that no one else in the city had, shots that no one could possibly have faked. There's going to be an investigation, I know that. But my bet is that the guy who called the Civic Pride Foundation won't show up when it's time for him to confront me and Peter face to face."

The publisher glared at Ben Urich, but Peter supposed he had to know that the experienced reporter was telling the truth. Meanwhile, Peter had his own theory about what had happened.

It's Venom, he thought. It has to be. Eddie Brock thinks that I ruined him when his story about the Sin-Eater was revealed as a hoax.

He lost his job, he lost his wife, and he lost his mind. Now he thinks that he can have revenge by making it look like I hoaxed the *Bugle*.

Everyone in the City Room was looking at Ben and Peter. Ben remained calm, but his mouth was set in a firm line. A vein was pulsing in J. Jonah Jameson's temple, and his cheeks were bright red. Peter wished he could just sink right through the floor.

"You get out of here!" Jameson shouted after another moment. "Both of you, just go! I'll get to the bottom of this, you can bet. Go!"

Relieved, Peter did just that.

Outside the City Room, Ben Urich caught up with Peter. He was walking slowly down the hall, trying to get his breathing under control. Fighting super-villains was nothing compared to the stress of facing the outspoken publisher of the *Daily Bugle*.

"Okay," Ben said as he joined Peter. "Want to go somewhere and talk for a minute?"

"Do I have a choice?" Peter asked bitterly.

"I suppose you do," Ben replied. "Everything in this life is a choice of one kind or another. You don't have to talk with me. But you know that I'm on your side in this."

Peter sighed. "Sure."

"Then let's go have a cup of coffee and a chat."

The two men, the reporter and the photographer, walked down the hall to the City Room's coffee machine.

"Here we are," Ben said a couple of minutes later. "I don't know about you, but I do my best thinking with a cup of Brazil's finest in my hand."

He poured himself a mug. "As I was saying," he continued after the first sip, "I don't think for a minute you faked any of those photos. For one reason: there was no need. We both saw things that were far more dramatic than anything anyone could have made up."

"The other reason," Peter said, "is that with the money J. Jonah pays, I couldn't afford to bribe anyone."

Ben laughed. "I suppose not. But listen, I'm serious. You have a bad habit of vanishing when the action starts, and reappearing after it's over with a stack of photos. No one else is ever around when you're doing your thing. That's got to cause talk. And when you showed up with a prize, maybe someone who was jealous . . . you get the idea? Someone wanted to hurt you, and that person chose a good way to do it. Do you have any enemies that you know of?"

That was a question that Peter didn't want to answer. As Peter Parker, no, he didn't have a lot of enemies. But as Spider-Man, he had too many. Only one person would think of trying to hurt Spider-Man by hurting Peter Parker: Eddie Brock, the one-time ace reporter now turned self-proclaimed protector of the innocent.

Watching Peter closely, Ben nodded. "I thought so," he said, as if he could read Peter's mind. Ben had been a reporter too long to be fooled by much. "Want to share who it is with me? Maybe I can help."

"As much as I want to," Peter said, "no. This is something I have to handle myself. Thanks."

"Sure," Ben said. "Don't forget my offer, though. Some things one man really can't handle all by himself. I've been writing about stuff like that all my life. And I don't want to have to write a news story about you, if you know what I mean. Now . . . how would you like to partner up again? This snow outside," Ben gestured with his hand to take in the whole city. "The weather forecasters are saying that it's shaping up to be the worst storm since the Great Blizzard of '88. *Eighteen*-eighty-eight, that is. There are stories out there, and I'm going to find some of them for the morning edition. Want to come along and take photos for me?"

What Ben was offering was exactly what Peter had hoped to get when he arrived at the *Bugle* building, and it was a real gesture of confidence coming now. Peter felt his face get hot with a surge of emotion.

"Thanks, Ben. But I don't think I can," he said with genuine regret. "Not right now. I know you'll come back with the goods, but you'd better choose another photographer. I'm probably a jinx around here at the moment."

"I think I know how you feel," Ben said kindly. "Take the rest of the night off. See you later. This'll all blow over. I'm sure of it." With that, the veteran reporter finished his coffee, shrugged on his coat, and walked off.

Peter finished his own coffee and headed back out into the streets, pondering the problem. There was no doubt in Peter's mind that Eddie Brock was behind this latest attack on his credibility. That would explain Venom's remarks down in the subway. But Peter couldn't shake the feeling that this was just the beginning of Venom's vengeance.

The wind was bitterly cold outside the *Bugle* building when Peter got down to the street. The snow came up to his knees in the drifts piled high by the stinging wind.

The street was choked with unmoving, empty cars. Their owners must have abandoned them, Peter thought, and gone looking for shelter elsewhere after the cars had bogged down.

"Everyone's indoors but me," Peter said out

loud, wrapping his arms tightly around himself. "Smart people."

Indoors seemed like a good place to head—indoors and home. But it looked like the city's taxis and buses were already out of the picture. Peter wondered how police, fire, and ambulance crews were going to manage. Even without any criminals on the streets, he realized unhappily, it looked like the kind of night when a super hero might be needed.

So much, he thought, for his own half-formed plan to head back to his apartment and ride out the storm in comfort with Mary Jane. He'd read a book once about the blizzard of 1888 that Ben had mentioned. That record-breaking storm had featured drifts of snow twenty feet deep in Manhattan. And people had frozen to death only a few feet away from their own doorsteps.

Peter sighed. *I have to get into costume and start web-slinging around,* he thought. *Peter Parker might be able to go home and wait for things to get better. Spider-Man can't allow himself the luxury.*

The decision made, Peter found a sheltered spot to shuck off his street clothes and pull on his spider suit. The head-to-toe action costume was a lot warmer than what he'd been wearing, and Spider-Man's outlook brightened considerably with the change.

Spidey stuffed his everyday clothing into the backpack that had carried the costume and stuck the pack twenty feet up on a wall with webbing. Then he was off and swinging.

His progress through the city was hard. He had to fight high winds that threatened to smash him into buildings as he swung past. His accuracy with the web-lines was also diminished. The wind tossed the lines around as they flew, making aiming each shot a separate, and difficult, exercise. The snow was blinding. After a while Spider-Man closed his eyes and continued swinging, letting his spider senses guide him. And while he swung, he thought.

Unless Spidey missed his guess, Venom was behind everything that had gone wrong today. He was convinced, though, that the bank robbery and the accusation of picture-faking weren't everything, or even the most important things, that Venom had planned. Given Venom's hatred for Spider-Man, they hadn't been nearly bad enough.

Whatever else he had planned, Venom's ultimate goal was eating Spidey's spleen. That much was a given. Something else, though, was going to come before that particular exercise. But what?

"Nice night for a swing," came a voice in Spider-Man's ear.

Spidey quickly looked side to side. He was

"Nice night for a swing," came a voice in Spider-Man's ear.

twenty stories up and moving fast. Who could it be? Then he saw the shadow beside him, matching him swing for swing. It was a huge black figure with a white spider design on chest and back. Inwardly, Spider-Man groaned.

"Won't you say hi to an old friend?" Venom asked. "I heard about the problems you had at the office. Too bad. Really. How does it feel to have everything you've worked for, your entire professional reputation, snatched away in an afternoon?"

"Eddie," Spider-Man said. "You know I didn't do that to you. I didn't force you to write that story about the Sin-Eater. I didn't lie to you—your source lied to you, not me. Can't you give it a rest?"

"Rest?" Venom answered, his voice mocking. He continued to match Spider-Man swing for swing, shooting web when Spidey shot, grinning his impossible fanged grin, his blank white eyes an evil parody of Spider-Man's own masked face. "Not until your *final* rest. You won't have long to wait for that. Not long at all."

And all at once Venom was gone, vanished into the storm. Spider-Man was left alone to swing through the gathering darkness. Twilight didn't last long under the storm clouds.

Still the snow came down, even heavier than before. And still the questions came.

What was Venom up to?

Every question led to another question.

Eddie Brock was no fool. Insane, perhaps. Dangerous, definitely. But no fool.

Keep your eyes open, Spider-Man reminded himself. With Venom after you, spider senses aren't going to be anywhere near enough to make you safe.

CHAPTER 6

SPIDER-MAN SWUNG west along 42nd Street. The winter storm made traveling by web-line hazardous, but he was going faster than he would have by any other method.

Traffic was at a standstill in the streets below. The George Washington Bridge had been closed due to high winds and blowing snow.

Department of Sanitation trucks mounted with snowplows were trying to clear away the drifts, and police department tow trucks were hard at work clearing the streets of abandoned cars—but they were losing ground.

From his vantage point high in the air, Spider-Man could see that even keeping open the main thoroughfares would soon become impossible. Before long, the plows wouldn't have any places left to put all the snow that they were clearing away.

I'm probably the only person in town right now who does *have an aerial view,* Spider-Man thought. Nobody with any sense was going to be out flying in this weather.

The major airports would have already shut down, most likely, stranding thousands of unhappy travelers in terminals and airport hotels. The roads going in and out of the city would be in bad shape as well. Visibility in the driving snow was close to zero, and the buffeting winds—topping eighty miles per hour, Spidey estimated, based on the way they were pushing him around—made flying totally unsafe.

Maybe Venom would abandon his vendetta in the face of the foul weather? And maybe pigs would grow wings and fly to Chicago, Spider-Man told himself. He couldn't count on Venom's peculiar idealism to save him—not when the super-villain's Spider-Man fixation was in full paranoid bloom.

Any respite gained from the storm would be a brief one, anyway. Venom would still be around tomorrow, and revenge would still be on his mind.

Not that Spidey was going to turn down a break if the storm gave him one. He'd fight Venom if he had to, but he wasn't planning to make a full-time occupation out of it.

A flash of bright orange-red off to the north attracted Spider-Man's attention. Looks like something's caught fire, he thought. And on a night like this, the emergency services would be hard-pressed getting anywhere.

He headed that way, or tried to. The wind was directly in his face, and his own weight wasn't enough to let him swing against it. He was being blown about like a kite on a string. He had to go lower where the wind wasn't so bad, and shoot a web-line directly ahead of him to use as an anchor.

He pulled himself along the anchoring line, using his spider-strength to fight his way against the wind. Down below him, in the wind-shadows of the multi-story buildings, the snowdrifts were already piled up higher than a man was tall.

No one's going anywhere tonight, he thought. Not unless they have to. And not without some kind of special gear.

The flash of orange-red came again, closer this time. Spider-Man laughed aloud with relief. The glow wasn't a fire after all—it was the Torch, making his way through the snow-filled air.

Spider-Man swung and pulled over to match the Torch's pace between the skyscrapers. The Torch was flying low and slow, scanning the city below.

Spider-Man swung and pulled over to match the Torch's pace between skyscrapers.

"What brings you out here?" Spider-Man called to his friend over the howl of the wind.

"Same things as you," the Torch replied. "Checking out the storm and looking for trouble spots. The city hasn't got anything that can fly in this soup." The Torch looked at Spider-Man for a moment as the web-slinger battled against the wind pulling on his lines. "Maybe we should team up."

"Sounds like a plan to me."

"We aren't too far from Four Freedoms Plaza," Torch said. "I was about to go in myself for a few minutes. We can work out our plans there."

Now that the Torch mentioned it, Spidey thought that a couple of minutes spent warming up and drying off might not be a bad idea. Even without Venom to worry about, this was shaping up to be a long night.

A few minutes later, Spidey and the Torch were inside the Fantastic Four's headquarters at Four Freedoms Plaza. Getting inside had been interesting: the Torch had to melt his way through a drift that blocked the way to the main door. Roof access might have been more convenient, but the winds up on that level made flying difficult and web-swinging all but impossible.

Except for the keening of the wind, the night was eerily silent. All the city's normal traffic noises were gone: no horns, no brakes, no wailing sirens. Just as the two super heroes entered the building, the street lights outside gave a flicker, then came back up. To Spider-Man they seemed to be slightly dimmer than before.

Johnny flamed off and entered the lobby. The companions went up the elevator. Once out, they were greeted by a cheery "Good evening," from the young blonde lady at the reception desk.

"Evening, Roberta," Johnny said. "Anything new?"

"There've been some serious problems with the power grid," the Fantastic Four's receptionist replied. "The building has switched over to alternate generators. Other than that," she consulted a list, "Reed called in. The problem the rest of the team has been dealing with is responding well. They should be back by tomorrow evening, so you should try to have the sonic gun repaired before then Also, the Wakandan embassy called to inquire. . . ."

The Fantastic Four were a busy and well-known super hero team. Roberta's report lasted several minutes. Spider-Man didn't pay much attention. He knew that Roberta was really an android, a robot constructed to appear human, and the business about reading a list was just a clever bit of programming designed to make her look more realistic to visitors.

"Thanks," Johnny said when Roberta had finished. "Keep your ears open for anything major in the city. Spider-Man and I are going to have a cup of coffee and maybe fiddle around with repairing the sonic gun before we head back out."

Spider-Man and the Torch went past Roberta and continued down the hall to one of the electronics labs. It was a brightly lit room with large windows that gave an impressive view of the Manhattan skyline. At least, most of the time it was impressive. Tonight the lights in the great skyscrapers were dim and indistinct, and the thick snow outside the window made the usually inspiring vista look like a close shot of the inside of a popcorn popper. The wind beat against the glass, making the panes vibrate.

The counters and worktables in the electronics lab were covered with parts bins and pieces of equipment: an oscilloscope and a square-wave generator; an assortment of circuit boards and coils of wire; a disassembled sonic gun; and an office-sized coffeemaker.

"Let me get the coffeepot going," Johnny said, pouring water into the top. "We never leave the thing on when no one's here. Coffee gets really nasty if it sits on the heat too long."

Spider-Man left Johnny making the fresh

coffee and took the opportunity to use the telephone to call Mary Jane.

The lab phone was in a separate alcove, and Spidey suspected that the Torch had made himself busy with the coffee on purpose, so that his masked-and-costumed guest could make a private call without revealing his secret identity. Maybe Johnny Storm had guessed the truth about Spider-Man a long time ago, and maybe not—but he was courteous enough not to pry into matters that a friend didn't want to reveal.

The phone call made Spider-Man feel better than he had in a while. Mary Jane Watson-Parker was home, warm, and safe. She'd checked on Aunt May, and all was well at May's home in Queens. There was lots of food in the house at both places, and the fuel tank at May's house had gotten filled up just the day before.

"I'm okay, honey," Spider-Man told his wife. "I'm staying downtown with Johnny Storm."

He didn't feel like telling her about the Civic Pride Foundation fiasco. Not now. Maybe the whole thing would be straightened out by tomorrow. Spidey could only hope. At least she hadn't asked him about Spider-Man supposedly robbing a bank. Maybe, if he was lucky, she hadn't seen the story. As for Venom—he'd tell her about *that* problem later, in person.

If I told her now, he reasoned, she'd only worry. And if I told her not to worry, that would just make her worry even more.

He went back into the other room, where the coffee was almost ready. It bubbled cheerily as it ran into the pot, filling the air with its warm, sharp smell. Spider-Man gratefully accepted a mug from the Torch and pulled his costume away from his mouth far enough to sip at the hot liquid.

Given a chance to warm up and dry out, Spidey was starting to cheer up again. Not even super-villains would be crazy enough to go out in weather that looked like it was going to break all the records for snowfall and wind-chill. And nobody at the Civic Pride Foundation was going to be investigating anything for a couple of days at least. Maybe by the time the storm blew itself out, he'd have figured a way to deal with his problems.

In the meantime, he had a chance to get back to doing the sort of thing that Spider-Man was good at—helping out people in trouble—without getting beaten up by anybody or anything except the weather.

The chiming of a bell interrupted his thoughts. Roberta's voice came into the lab over a hidden speaker.

"Mr. Storm, there's a delivery man here. He says he's from Tocsin Industries, and that what he has must be delivered in person."

"Tocsin Industries?" Johnny looked puzzled. "I don't recall ordering anything from any firm by that name."

"No real delivery man's going to be out tonight," Spider-Man said. "I smell something fishy going on here."

"So do I," Johnny said. "Nothing that the two of us can't handle, though. And I'm kind of curious as to what this is all about." He turned back to the intercom.

"Let him in, Roberta."

"Here he comes," Roberta replied.

A few moments later the laboratory door clicked open. The light from outside was blocked momentarily as the delivery man came in. He was a big man, with a weight-lifter's body. He almost filled the doorway from side to side and from top to bottom. Then the fellow stepped forward into the light, and Spider-Man saw at once who it was: Eddie Brock, dressed in the uniform of a parcel delivery service and carrying a case in one hand.

Eddie put the case down on the workbench next to the disassembled sonic gun. "I knew that you'd want to have this tonight," he said.

Johnny Storm looked at Eddie Brock and

then at Spider-Man. "Friend of yours?" he asked, his voice carefully casual.

Johnny is stalling for time, Spider-Man thought. *He knows Brock by sight but he's letting me decide how I want to handle this. I'm grateful . . . I think.*

"Maybe a friend and maybe not," Spider-Man said. "It all depends on what he's got in the box."

"I'm wounded," Eddie said. "You know that I only want what's best for you. Fried onions, for example."

"Fried onions?" Spider-Man asked, puzzled.

Eddie Brock grinned—a normal human grin that nevertheless made Spidey think of white fangs and a long, slime-dripping tongue. "They go well with liver, or so I hear. Anybody's liver."

He left the case where he'd put it down and walked over to the coffeepot.

"Mind if I have some? It's cold outside, and I've been too busy to pick up a cup."

"Help yourself," Johnny said. "Just don't touch the cups with the blue rims, okay? They belong to the Thing, and he gets really upset if somebody else drinks out of them."

"Wouldn't dream of it," Eddie said. "You know I have nothing but the greatest respect for the Fantastic Four." He picked out a mug, filled it, and added cream and sugar. "I don't see how anyone can stand to drink this stuff black."

"Eddie," Spider-Man said, "I don't think that you're here on a social call. So what's the point?"

"I heard you were short of cash," Eddie said. He took a sip of the coffee. "This is really good," he said to Johnny. "Where do you buy your coffee—and do you get it ground or do you grind it yourself?"

"The *box*, Eddie," Johnny said. "Tell us what's in the box."

Spidey was glad to see that Eddie Brock's attempt at light conversation wasn't fooling the Torch. While Brock could be gentle, kind, and friendly when it suited him—even heroic in an odd kind of way when he was defending helpless innocents—those times never came while Spider-Man was in the same room.

"Oh, yes," said Eddie. "The box. It's got the money that was stolen from the Seaforth Trust this afternoon. Hundreds of witnesses saw Spider-Man take it, so it's only right that he should have it now."

CHAPTER 7

IS ALL THE MONEY in that box?" Spider-Man asked. Returning the stolen cash could be embarrassing, especially if he had to prove his innocence in the process. But it was still something that had to be done.

"No," Brock replied. He took another sip of his coffee. "Only about half."

"Where's the rest of it?"

"Someplace where the police will find it. If it wasn't for all this bad weather they'd have recovered it already, but I understand that they're a little busy."

"The bad weather," Spider-Man said, "is not my fault."

"For once I agree," Eddie said. "So there *is* one thing, after all, that you don't claim credit for."

Eddie was keeping calm, but Spider-Man could see that the effort was costing him. For an instant the symbiote appeared—manifesting itself on Brock's left wrist in a black, whiplike flicker, then darting back and blending into the jacket sleeve.

Spider-Man noted the symbiote's sudden vanishing act. Eddie Brock was trying hard to keep his rage under control, and that by itself was enough to make Spider-Man uneasy.

All that unnatural calmness could only mean that Venom wanted to do something that he needed to stay calm for, something that he couldn't accomplish if he gave in to blind rage. Spider-Man tried to imagine what sort of something that might be.

The possibilities weren't encouraging. Venom was dangerous enough already. Tempering his hatred with restraint would only serve to make him worse.

Just my luck, Spidey said to himself. My enemies get saner, and all it does is improve their aim.

The thought gave him an idea. Maybe the best bet would be *not* to calm Venom down, but to do exactly the reverse. It was a risky move, but Spidey was as well placed to make it right now as he'd ever be. He and the Torch, working together, had defeated Venom before.

Of course, he and the Torch had been lucky.

And so far today, Spider-Man's luck had not been good.

"So what if the police get the money back?" he asked out loud. "I *want* the police to get the money back. I'm going to be giving them this bundle of cash myself, as soon as they aren't distracted by the weather any more."

"What's the first thing that anyone's going to do when that money comes in?" Eddie Brock asked. His manner was still pleasant and sociable, although the tension in his jaw and in the corded muscles of his neck showed that he was under considerable strain. "They'll check it and the box it was in for fingerprints."

"No one has a sample of my fingerprints," Spidey said. He held up his gloved hand and waggled his fingers.

"No, I suppose no one does," Eddie agreed. "I think that maybe the fingerprints will belong to someone else, a college student maybe, or some other ordinary guy. He might even have a part-time job somewhere. The police will track him down. Come to his apartment with a search warrant, poke around in his closet. Do you suppose they'll find a red-and-blue costume hanging there? Imagine that young man's pretty wife in tears as he's led away in handcuffs. Imagine her filing for divorce. That sort of thing happens to people, you know. Or maybe the cops will go to his place of employment. How do you think his boss will react to the news that one of his free-lancers—"

"Watch it!" the Torch said sharply.

"No, *you* watch it!" Brock roared. His face grew red, and a vein began to pulse in his neck. In the next instant, his massive body was encased in gleaming black and white as the deliveryman's uniform he wore morphed into Venom's distinctive garb. Pointed fangs clashed. The coffee mug he held disintegrated as a clawed hand crushed it into powder. "And *you* stay out of this!"

A second later Eddie Brock was back in control, and the symbiote had vanished, morphing again into ordinary clothing. Brock no longer wore the delivery service uniform, however; his clothing now was a jacket and jeans, and a tee-shirt with a funny slogan. He turned back to Spider-Man as though the moment of transformation had never happened.

"You probably want to know who's been committing these crimes in your name," Brock said. His voice was calm, but the barely suppressed rage still burned in his eyes.

Good, thought Spider-Man. Stay angry. Get angrier.

"Well, yes," Spidey admitted. "I've given it a thought or two in my spare time."

"As it happens," Brock said, "I've got an inside track on that particular question. Are you interested?"

Spidey shrugged. He deliberately made the gesture as insulting as possible. "It depends. Is your, um, *source* any better this time than it was before?"

The veiled reference to the false Sin-Eater worked as Spider-Man had hoped it would. The anger flared up even higher in Brock's eyes—but his control held, at least for the moment.

"My source is good. In fact," Brock said, "my source is perfect. Do you recall that last group of super-villains you caught—the Sinister Six? They're in holding cells down at Manhattan Criminal Court, waiting for the grand jury to finish with them." Brock paused. "And what I hear from my source is that Spider-Man is secretly a member of the same group."

There was another pause. Then the Torch looked over at Spider-Man. "That's news to me."

"Me, too," said Spider-Man. He looked back at Eddie Brock. "Sorry, Eddie, your 'source' is making up his facts. Again."

Eddie Brock grinned. "You'll know better when you read the story tomorrow, with photos. I heard that Spider-Man is going to reveal his true allegiance at midnight."

CHAPTER 8

"YOU ALREADY KNOW my true allegiance, Eddie," Spider-Man said. "I protect people. I stop crooks."

Eddie sneered at him. "You think I believe that?"

"What I believe," Spider-Man said, "is that you're a genuine nutcase."

This time Eddie didn't rise to the insult. But the muscle twitching in his jaw twitched faster, and his massive fists clenched tight with the effort of maintaining control.

Good, Spider-Man thought. It's working. If he has a plan, maybe I can get him mad enough to ditch it and take the direct route instead. All this devious stuff is new for Venom, and I'm not sure that I like it.

In fact, Spidey thought, I'm sure that I don't.

Time to twist the screws a little tighter, then. Spider-Man hoped that the Torch had guessed enough of his strategy to be ready for action when Venom's lid blew off.

"I do know one thing," Spidey told Eddie Brock. "You're trying to *look* like Spider-Man because you can't *be* him. You wish that you were Spider-Man . . . and that alien suit of yours probably wishes that you were Spider-Man, too."

"Shut up!" Eddie yelled. "Don't talk about my other that way!"

Again the alien symbiote flowed over Eddie Brock, and this time it didn't flow away again. Venom's many-fanged jaw gaped impossibly wide, and his lashing tongue threw spittle.

"We've heard enough, Spider-Man!" the creature shouted. "Now we will crush your bones and use your skull for an egg cup!"

Spider-Man ducked the flying spray of greenish slime. "Believe it or not," he called out to Johnny Storm, "I was hoping that this would happen!"

After that, he was too busy for conversation. Venom was on Spider-Man in one long, low leap. All pretense of calm abandoned, the man-and-symbiote combination drew back a fist and smashed it into the place where Spider-Man had been standing.

Spidey dropped and rolled on the floor as the blow came in. He kicked up with both legs, driving his feet into Venom's ribs.

The black-clad super-villain looked as startled as possible for a creature with a foot-long slavering tongue to look. He flew backward over a workbench, accompanied by the sound of smashing equipment.

The greater part of Spider-Man's attention was taken up by Venom, but not so much of it that he could miss hearing Johnny Storm's cry of "Flame on!"

A red glow filled the room, and the temperature went up by several degrees. Venom ripped up the workbench he had just sailed over, and swung it hard, aiming for the Torch.

"Unfair—but we are still more than a match for the two of you!"

The blow missed, but only because the Torch retreated in time for the bench to go swinging past him. Venom let go of the bench at the end of its arc, so that it went flying through the air at Spider-Man instead.

"One of you or both of you. It makes no difference to us!" Venom said as the bench hurtled toward Spider-Man.

Spidey leapt for the ceiling to avoid the impromptu missile. As he jumped, an unearthly scream pierced the air.

Looking down, he saw that the Human Torch had grappled Venom from behind. The symbiote had as much of an aversion to heat as it did to sonics—both caused it pain. A moment later, Venom twisted and flung the Torch through the air to smack flat against the far wall. The Torch's impact left a burn mark on the paint.

Spidey took advantage of Venom's momentary distraction to plant a web-line on the far wall and slide down along it. He planted his fist on Venom's jaw, narrowly missing the snapping fangs, and made the bigger man reel back several feet.

"That does it!" Venom shouted. "Now you're ours!" He grasped Spider-Man's wrist, pulled hard, and threw Spidey to the floor in a fast arc.

Spidey rolled to his right to avoid the smashing blow that Venom threw at him. "Sorry—not just yet."

The Torch was back on his feet. He landed a flaming kick on Venom's ribs that peeled the symbiote away from the human flesh beneath. "No rest for the wicked," the Torch said. "Not in this fight."

"Who are you calling wicked?" Venom snarled, twisting away from the attack and sending out symbiotic streamers to pull part of the ceiling down on the Torch. Scraps of plasterboard and metal stripping flew everywhere. As the dust settled, Spidey saw that a steel beam now pinned Johnny to the floor.

Venom turned his full attention to Spider-Man. But Spider-Man had not been idle. As soon as he saw Venom take down the Torch, he ran, jumped, and turned a handspring into a devastating double-footed kick.

Venom wasn't prepared for the impact—it drove him to the floor. Then it was Spider-Man's turn to throw a swing at Venom's face. Venom caught Spider-Man's fist in his hand.

"Violence on television causes this sort of thing," he remarked. He pushed upward, bending Spider-Man's arm back and back. "We're stronger than you," Venom said. "Here comes the end."

"Not quite!" came the shout from across the room. With a sudden, intense burst, the Torch melted through the steel beam that trapped him.

The flame was strong enough to set off the sprinklers in the room. A rain of cold water began to drench the laboratory.

The blast of heat had also made the symbiote on Venom's flank peel away in ragged black shreds. Spider-Man took the opportunity to batter his opponent a few more times.

"Is there a problem?" The artificial voice of Roberta echoed in the room. "Shall I summon the fire department?"

"Everything's . . . under . . . control," Johnny panted. The sprinklers weren't enough to extinguish his fire, although he needed more energy than usual to stay aflame. He joined Spider-Man in his assault on Venom. The black-clad super-villain was forced steadily backward, deeper into the room, farther from the exit.

"We've got him—" Spider-Man shouted, just as Venom turned and, with a mighty leap, smashed through the glass window to hurtle away into the howling snowstorm beyond.

"—cornered," Spidey finished lamely. He sagged to the floor in frustrated exhaustion.

A blast of cold and snow filled the room. Spidey started to shiver as the arctic wind met his soggy costume, drenched anew by the fire sprinklers.

"Let him go," Johnny said, flaming off. "You can't track him in this weather. We need to shut off the fire sprinklers anyway, then get the window sealed before we have ten-foot snowdrifts piled up in here."

"I suppose you're right," said Spider-Man. "Let's get to work."

While Johnny Storm turned off the sprinklers, Spidey hunted out a roll of plastic from

Venom turned and, with a mighty leap, smashed through the glass window to hurtle away into the howling snowstorm beyond.

the supply closet. By using Spider-Man's webbing for a temporary adhesive and Johnny's flames for tack welding, the two super heroes managed to wrestle a flapping sheet of heavy-duty plastic across the broken window and seal it in place.

That emergency repair taken care of, Johnny and Spider-Man paused to catch their breath and look around at the wreckage. Super hero/super-villain combat sure could wreck a place, Spider-Man thought. The workbench was in splinters, part of the ceiling was on the floor, the walls had water stains where they didn't have scorch marks, and the coffeepot was shattered into bits.

Johnny Storm held up a broken coffee mug with a blue band. "Oh, heck, look at this. The Thing is really going to be upset." He put the broken mug back down on the counter and looked over at Spider-Man. "So tell me—what were we fighting about, anyway?"

"Venom's trying to ruin me," Spidey answered. "He's got some kind of plan where, even if I survive, my reputation will be in such a mess that I'll never work in this town again."

Johnny pointed at the case of money. Whether by coincidence or by Venom's design, it still lay untouched on the counter where

Eddie Brock had put it. "Is that why he left that stuff here?"

"Probably," said Spider-Man. "Venom wants me to check the money to prove that he isn't bluffing. If I check it, I'll probably find out that the cash was all really stolen from the Seaforth Bank, and that the bills all have my real—I mean, my secret persona's—fingerprints on them."

The Torch looked puzzled. "How can he do that?"

"Eddie Brock can't," said Spidey. "But the symbiote can do it for him. At least, I suspect that it can. The creature's intimately familiar with my biology, including my fingerprints. It was molded to my body, fingers and all, and I'll bet that it remembers. So all the symbiote had to do was rearrange a part of itself into the loops and whorls on my own personal fingertips while Venom handled the case and the bills."

"Clever," said the Torch. "He's not a guy that I'd like to have after me, I can tell you that much. So what are you going to do about this?"

"Venom mentioned that something would be going on down at the Manhattan Criminal Courts building at midnight," Spider-Man said. "I'll be there."

"Let me give you a word of advice," the Torch said. "Listen to your Uncle Johnny: I think that it would be a really dumb idea for you to go to that meeting. Venom has got something planned, and selling you magazine subscriptions probably isn't it. Why don't you let me go to the rendezvous instead?"

"No, I think I have to be there," Spider-Man said. What he didn't say out loud was that even if he didn't show up as Spider-Man, he'd still want to be on the scene as Peter Parker, news photographer. Someone had to get proof that Venom was behind Spider-Man's latest problems, and he couldn't rely on anyone else providing it for him.

"I can't talk you out of going?" the Torch asked.

"No. Venom's my problem, not yours. I have to take care of him myself. And one thing is certain—whatever Venom has got planned, *somebody* has to try and stop it."

"Okay, Spidey," the Torch said. "Then what do you say to the two of us going together? Safety in numbers, and all that."

"All right. One other thing you can do for me—do you have a camera around here that I can borrow?"

"Sure," Johnny said. "And you can help me finish repairing that broken sonic gun. If we're going to be dealing with Venom, we're going to need it."

"I have a better idea," Spider-Man said. "Why don't you call the Vault, the federal prison for super-villains. Ask them to send a containment vehicle here to pick up Venom. We know where he'll be, we'll catch him in the act, and we'll put him where he belongs."

"Sounds reasonable to me," Johnny said. He made a phone call.

A few minutes later, he hung up. "They've got a pick-up team on the way," Johnny said. "With the weather, though, they can't make it until after midnight."

"We'll just have to hold Venom until they show up," Spider-Man said. "Let's get back to work on that sonic gun."

CHAPTER 9

THE TWO SUPER HEROES set to work. As a physics student in his other life, Spider-Man understood the theory and the techniques of electronic and mechanical repair. And while he was nowhere near as good as Johnny Storm at working on the Fantastic Four's gear, he still knew which end of a soldering iron to hold.

Johnny began reassembling the pieces of the sonic gun. The weapon had proved useful in past fights with Venom. Spider-Man hoped that it would prove equally useful tonight. While the Torch worked on the gun, Spidey took one of the Fantastic Four's cameras and rigged it for automatic action in low light levels. As he worked, he thought about his problems.

Journalism, with its trafficking in rumors and reputations, was the key to everything that had happened so far—that much was clear. Once, Eddie Brock had been a first-class reporter. And Spider-Man, as Peter Parker, worked at the heart of the newspaper business. It looked as if Venom, with his strong but warped sense of justice, planned to use the power of the press to bring Spider-Man down.

Spidey almost laughed. Didn't Venom know that the publisher of the *Daily Bugle*, circulation five million, already tried to bring down Spider-Man every day?

No, Spider-Man decided, probably not. Or if Venom knew, he didn't care.

And in spite of his prejudice against Spider-Man, J. Jonah Jameson had never tried to manipulate the news and create a story. However slanted his approach might be, he still stuck to the truth as his reporters saw it. But tomorrow, with Venom's plan running at full speed, who could tell what kind of headlines the *Bugle* would run?

Spider-Man had an uncomfortable feeling that he knew all too well.

"Tell me," he said, looking up from clipping wire ends from the back of a circuit board. "Do you think that Venom will really reveal my secret identity?"

"He knows it?"

"He knows everything that there is to know about me," Spider-Man said.

"Then what's been stopping him from going up to a phone booth any time he wanted to, dropping a coin in the slot, and calling up the wire services with the story, 'Spider-Man's Real Name Revealed?'"

"Nothing," Spider-Man admitted. "Except that Venom doesn't work that way."

"Then how does he work?" the Torch asked, a bit confused. "What's he after, if just letting the word get out isn't enough for him?"

"He wants," Spider-Man said, "to eat my spleen. Literally. Sometimes other body parts, but he always keeps coming back to spleens."

"So this entire affair is an attempt to put you in a time and place in which he can eat your spleen?"

"No," said Spider-Man after a moment's thought. "That can't be it either. Whatever Venom is up to needs more thought than that. He doesn't just want me dead—he wants me to suffer first."

"Well, then," Johnny admitted, "I'm baffled." He tightened a last miniature screw on the stock of the sonic gun. "Speaking of baffles—let's go downstairs to the practice range so I can test the heat baffles on this thing. If I can't use it in Flame On mode, then it's not going to do me much good."

The gun tested out okay, and so did the

jury-rigged camera. When the tests were done, they checked the clock. It was 11:30.

"Time to go," Spider-Man said. "I don't want to be late for this midnight party Venom's holding in my honor."

"I can't convince you not to go?"

"Nope. Suppose he had ice cream and cake, and I didn't show?"

Together Spider-Man and the Torch left the building. Johnny Storm had the sonic gun slung behind him. Spider-Man wore the camera around his neck.

When they got to the street, they saw that the weather had gotten even worse during the hours they'd spent in cleanup and tinkering. Signs rattled as the wind tore at them. The air was so full of snow it seemed almost solid. The street lights created dim, cone-shaped areas of illumination in the dense, swarming whiteness. There was no sound anywhere other than the moaning wind. Stalled vehicles were buried in great mounds of snow along the sides of the street, and the snow on the sidewalks had blown into drifts higher than Spider-Man's head.

"I don't think we're going to get far by calling a taxi," Spidey observed.

"Flame on!" Johnny shouted, blazing up into the middle of the air. "That cuts the chill nicely," he called down to Spider-Man. "But it's a lousy night for flying."

Spider-Man shot a web-line to a fire escape in an alley on the other side of the street. "This isn't going to be easy," he said as he climbed up the line to get some altitude. "Let's get going. Venom isn't going to hold up the show on account of bad road conditions."

The two super heroes started on their way. Hurricane-strength gusts of wind made their progress difficult. The wind and biting snow kept visibility down to almost nil. Only their excellent knowledge of the city, as they counted cross streets and watched for landmarks, enabled them to find their way at all.

The wind caught the snow that had already fallen. It blew it in white sheets across the night, adding it to the flakes that were still falling to create a blinding screen.

Spider-Man swung from building to building, using the anchor-lines he had figured out during the earlier hours of the storm.

Then something on the street below drew Spider-Man's attention. Down in the drifting snow, he spotted a dark dot in an otherwise unbroken layer of white. The dot was moving.

"What's that?" Spider-Man shouted to the Torch. He had to shout twice more before the Torch could hear him. In weather like this, the falling snow deadened whatever sound the wind didn't carry away.

"Don't know!" the Torch called back.

"I'm going to check it out," Spidey said. He let go of his web-line and plummeted to the street. Only a few feet above the blanket of snow, he shot a web-line to a nearby building. The line checked his fall, and converted his momentum into a swing to the dark spot he had noticed a moment before.

He swung fast above the spot, then back up to where the Torch hovered in mid-air.

"People!" Spider-Man shouted as he came near the Torch. "Stuck out in the storm."

"We can't leave them out here," the Torch said. "They'll freeze for sure."

"Elevator going down," Spidey said. Again he plunged, this time landing lightly in the place he had spotted.

The snow here was deeper than Spidey was tall. Something, though, had made a depression in the snow, a kind of circular hollow. Inside the hollow were a group of people. Spidey counted ten of them. These were harmless street people, the derelict and homeless. Winter was never a good time for them, and on a night like tonight, being homeless could mean being dead real fast.

After looking at them for a moment, Spidey realized that the hollow had been created and was being kept in place by three of the men—walking, endlessly walking, circling the others, pushing back the snow with their bodies. The other people huddled in the center of the depression on the hard-packed white, trying to keep warm. One was a child; she was crying. All of them were too exhausted even to register surprise at one of Manhattan's super heroes dropping in on them from out of the sky.

"How's it going?" Spider-Man asked.

"Been worse," said one of the walkers. "Before the walls got high enough, the snow was blowing pretty good. But now we're out of the wind."

Spidey looked at the precarious wall of snow looming above their heads. "You're in danger of being buried."

"Can't help that," another of the circling men said. "Where'd you come from, anyway?"

"Just dropped in. You folks want to go somewhere warm and dry?"

"Yeah, now that you mention it," said the first man. "Ralphie and Buster and me, we're getting a little tired. Time for you to take your turn while we get some sleep."

"No, not sleep," Spider-Man said. "You'll freeze to death. Look, I think there's a shelter about a block from here. It'll be warm in there, and they'll have food. There'll be people and light. What do you say?"

The one called Ralphie shook his head wearily. "Man, I hate to tell you, but there's no way to get there from here. Look around you, man."

"Honest—there's a way. Hey, Johnny!"

The Torch came down to hover just overhead. The glow of the red flames coming off his body showed how thin, wet, and poorly dressed for the weather Ralphie and the others were.

"What do you need me to do?" he called down to Spider-Man.

"How would you like to melt a path for these folks?" Spidey shouted back up at him. They both had to yell to make themselves heard over the wind. "Take them over to the Baptist Mission on Eighth Avenue?"

"Sure thing."

"Okay," Spider-Man said to the group of people.

"It's time to take a walk. You know how mountain climbers go, when they're crossing snowfields—they tie themselves together so no one gets lost? Well, that's what we're going to do. We're going to rope ourselves together with some of my web.

"Spiderweb? Oh yech," one of the women said. Her breath smelled heavily of wine.

"No, Spider-*Man* web. It's different," Spidey said in his calmest voice. "Ready? Everyone up. We're not going to lose anyone or leave anyone behind."

"Coming in," the Torch said, landing a little bit away from the group. Then: "Come on. This way."

The Torch burned a little brighter, it seemed, as he pushed into the side of the icy cliff. He took a pace forward, and the snow melted away before him.

Fresh flakes fell on them, the wind screamed above them, but the Torch paced steadily forward. Spider-Man followed a careful distance behind, shielding the others from the flames with his body, for the Torch was both bright and hot.

Spidey took another step forward. The snow the Torch was melting turned to water. The water mixed with snow and turned to slush under his feet. In less than a minute, the slush was freezing solid again.

They moved along as quickly as they could. Still, the group wasn't going to reach their goal by midnight.

"I can't afford to be late," Spider-Man said.

"You go ahead," the Torch replied "I'll get these folks to safety and be along as quickly as I can."

"Sorry I can't stay," Spidey said as he shot a web-line above him and swung into the night. "I have an appointment."

Fresh flakes fell on them, the wind screamed above them, but the Torch paced steadily forward.

CHAPTER 10

THE MANHATTAN CRIMINAL COURT building was, as Spider-Man had expected, thoroughly snow covered by the time he arrived. In the open street, the wind whipping over the flat ground had scoured the snow down to about three feet. It was waist deep, but not impossible to get through. Wherever a solid object thrust up, the wind had deposited drifts. The snow had piled up in wind-sculpted dunes and mountains around the mailboxes and the fire hydrants, around and on top of the ranks of abandoned cars, and around a deserted bus stalled halfway down the block. In the drifts, and along the downwind sides of the buildings, the snow was twenty to thirty feet deep.

The first thing to do, Spidey thought, is find the fake Spider-Man and get this over with.

But he knew it wouldn't be easy. The whiteout conditions caused by the wind and the blowing snow limited visibility enough to make finding anyone difficult.

But it would not be impossible. The absence of people and moving vehicles would make it easier to spot anything out of the ordinary. Anyone moving, anyone leaving tracks, would be obvious. Not that Venom, whether in his own guise or disguised as a fake Spider-Man, would leave tracks. Venom was as proficient at web-slinging and wall-crawling as Spider-Man was himself.

Clinging to the sheltered side of a nearby building, Spidey slowly scanned the streets below . . . and saw something.

An object was moving at street level, something with lights. He swung lower to see what it might be.

It was a snowmobile—a small, open vehicle with two skis on the front and a fast-moving wide track in the rear. Normally such machines were used for wintertime sport riding in the northern woods, but this one was speeding down the middle of the otherwise impassable street.

Somebody's sure clever, Spider-Man thought. He wondered who it could be, and made a low pass to see if he could recognize the snowmobile's driver.

He could. It was Albert van Tahn, a reporter for the *Daily Globe*. His passenger was Connie Castaigne, a *Globe* photographer.

She was quick, too. As Spider-Man passed within five feet of the duo, her camera's flash strobed out, catching Spidey in mid-swing.

Spider-Man continued on to the wall of a building opposite the courthouse, where he stuck and waited until the snowmobile passed by. It didn't continue far. In the square surrounding the courthouse and its prison-like complex of holding cells, the reporter and photographer came to a halt. In the deep shadow of a building, they shut off their lights and waited.

This isn't right, Spider-Man thought. I wonder what's up? What were they doing out in the storm? The last Spidey had heard, Bertie was handling the crime beat for the *Globe*.

Then it hit him. The reporter and photographer were waiting for a crime. They'd been tipped off about whatever the false Spider-Man was about to do. Spidey was anxious to find the answer to that question himself.

He supposed that he could ask Bertie. That might be bad form, though—if J. Jonah Jameson ever found out that a *Bugle* employee had to go to the *Globe* to get news, it would be worse than if he found out that one of his employees was Spider-Man.

Suddenly a siren began to wail. It sounded muted and far away in the thick snow. Spidey froze, concentrating all of his senses to try to find the source. There—it was the siren at the prison! Buffeted by the winds, he headed over to the jail. Some desperate criminals were locked up in there, including some that he'd had a hand in collecting. The prospect of these villains escaping and commiting new crimes made it imperative that he act immediately.

The doors of the prison came open and light spilled out, along with several policemen. Some wore blue parkas, others were in uniform jackets, and still others hadn't had time to put on anything over their winter shirts. Spider-Man swung down to the nearest door and perched on the wall above it. His worst fears were confirmed—it was indeed a jailbreak.

Just as I figured, Spidey thought. Venom is probably in there right now, dressed as Spider-Man, ripping doors off of cells. The symbiote menace had to be stopped!

Spider-Man quickly unlimbered the camera he'd borrowed from the Fantastic Four and webbed it to the wall. He set it to automatically snap pictures, using low-light film. Then he gripped the top of the door and swung down inside the building. He was greeted with a scene of total confusion, with police barking orders, sirens blasting, and prisoners running every which way.

Spider-Man proceeded down a hallway, where he was momentarily alone.

And then he came face to face with his double, or someone who would have been his double if Spider-Man looked like a body builder when he wasn't wearing his costume.

"Oh, good, you made it," said the fake Spider-Man. And in an instant the red-and-blue costume morphed and he became Eddie Brock, wearing a police uniform.

"Courting a little damage to my personal, unprotected skin," Brock said. "Well worthwhile, I'd call it. Now, let's take this outside."

Spider-Man shot a web at Eddie. Eddie rolled under it, and popped up in Spider-Man's face.

"I'm faster than you, and lots stronger," Eddie said.

With that he grabbed Spider-Man's hand, pulled it to his chest, and leapt backward into the squad room. To anyone watching, it would have looked like Spider-Man had grabbed a cop by the shirt and pushed him in from the hall. Brock let go of Spider-Man's hand, and ran out the open door.

Spider-Man followed and grabbed him around the legs, bringing Brock to the ground.

"What's the matter?" Brock whispered as

they landed together in the snow. "Why aren't you hitting us?"

"Because you want me to," Spider-Man said.

"That's what we were counting on. But here, I'll help you."

A tendril of black symbiotic substance sprang out, almost invisible in the dark and the blowing snow. It grasped Spider-Man's hand by the wrist, and pulled it forward to make a smacking contact with Eddie Brock's jaw.

The blow wasn't hard, but Brock acted as if it were. He snapped his head back and yelled as if in pain.

"The thing is," Brock whispered, while his face and eyes still expressed great fear, "when my other isn't covering us completely, there's a lot of its substance left over. Enough of it to make you dance like a puppet on strings."

Another tendril flew out and wrapped around Spider-Man's ankle. It pulled his leg forward to kick Brock in the ribs.

"I won't let you do this," Spider-Man protested.

"You don't have a choice," Eddie said. "You're doing it."

Spider-Man's left wrist was pulled forward in what looked like a vicious blow to Brock's midriff. Eddie hammed it up by doubling over as if he'd been hurt. Spidey tried to break away from the symbiote's grip. But he was distracted by a sudden thought: The *Globe* photographer must be shooting this! I wonder where she is? In that moment of hesitation, Spidey's wrist was once again seized and pulled in to appear as though he'd punched the poor policeman in the jaw.

What's so frustrating about this, Spidey thought, is that I'd really love to beat the stuffing out of Brock, but I can't do it now.

Brock threw himself back as though punched, landed on his back in the snow and lay still. Then Venom's powerful tendrils grabbed Spider-Man and pulled him into a high arc, letting him land on Brock so that it looked as if Spidey were jumping on a defenseless policeman.

While he was in mid-air, Spidey saw the flash of a camera. He looked and saw Connie Castaigne with her camera at her eye, getting all the details of Spider-Man in action, leaping on his victim.

"Seems like there's only one way out of this," Spider-Man said as he landed on the disguised Venom. "If I really beat you and hand you over to the police, then your plot will be exposed, you'll go back to jail, and I'll be off the hook."

"You want to take that gamble? You've

The blow wasn't hard, but Brock acted as if it were. He snapped his head back, and yelled as if in pain.

never beaten me in hand-to-hand fighting before."

"I feel lucky tonight," Spider-Man said, with the desperation of one who's run out of options.

"Then let's see you take your best shot," Venom said. He jutted forth his chin as if daring Spider-Man to punch him.

The flashes of the camera came quicker. Spidey noticed that through it all, Brock was keeping his face turned away from the photographer.

He doesn't dare get his real face shown while he's pretending to be one of Manhattan's finest, Spidey thought. *That's an advantage for me.*

But not much of an advantage. Spider-Man slammed into Brock, and the two of them went down in a tangle of arms and legs in the midst of a snowdrift. In that whirl of cold white Spidey lost his grip on Venom. The super hero clambered out of the drift and shook his head clear. When he looked around he saw that Venom, now dressed as Spider-Man, was pummeling a group of startled policemen.

As Venom spotted Spider-Man, he quickly shot a line of webbing and pulled himself up into the darkness. He dropped beside Spidey and shook the snow from himself. At the same moment, the symbiote turned itself into the outer clothing of an ordinary citizen.

Then, hidden for the moment from Connie Castaigne's camera, he swung his fist at Spider-Man and connected. Spidey twisted to lessen the impact. He knew what kind of power Eddie Brock packed in his arms. He was surprised that the blow didn't hurt more. Brock must be pulling his punches, he thought. But why?

Spider-Man counterpunched, his fist landing just as another camera flash explode. The *Globe* now had a great shot of Spider-Man striking an unarmed civilian.

"What about the crooks you let loose?" Spider-Man asked as Eddie grappled with him. "Don't you worry about what kind of crimes they'll commit, victimizing innocent people, before they're caught again?"

"Not really," Brock replied, hitting Spider-Man with a punishing one-two combination hidden from the camera's eye. "On a night like tonight, how far are they going to get, anyway? Besides," he added, rocking Spider-Man back with a smash to the abdomen, "they were in the holding cells, waiting for arraignment. This is America—they're still innocent until proven guilty."

"I never thought you'd be that big a supporter of the judicial system," Spider-Man said.

"Oh, I *am*," Brock assured him. "After all, I was convicted and sent to prison by the judicial system, and we both know that I'm innocent of any crime." He ducked under Spider-Man's punch. "Other than trying to kill you, of course. But that isn't a crime. It's a public service."

"That isn't going to help you," Spidey said. He spun a quick web around Brock's wrist and twisted him toward the lights. "Let's show you to the cameras."

"Let's not," Brock said. "I think it's time for you to fight the police again."

He threw himself forward into the trampled snow, hiding from the photographer and reporter before they could see his face or get his picture. Spider-Man turned to see Eddie Brock once again in police uniform, standing in front of him. This was one officer Spider-Man was happy to hit, and he did so.

"Why did you want me here, anyway?" Spider-Man asked. "Wouldn't it have been easier for you to do your fake routine without me?"

"And risk having you turn up fighting a fire on 123rd Street? With the fire commissioner, the mayor, a TV news crew, and four hundred solid citizens as witnesses that you were somewhere else at the time? No. I had to have you where I could control you."

Once more the black tendrils whipped out, taking Spider-Man's arms and legs in their grip. Overhead, the streetlights flickered, and this time they went out.

Where *is* the Torch? Spider-Man wondered, as the symbiote drew him forward into combat once more. He should have been here by now with that sonic gun. Because if I ever needed something to stop Venom in a hurry, now's the time.

CHAPTER 11

AS THE WIND WHIPPED and howled around the darkened square, Eddie Brock pulled Spider-Man in close.

"You've tried that trick already," Spider-Man said. "And no one can see what's happening now. The lights are out, so what you look like doesn't make any difference."

Spidey didn't feel anywhere near as confident as he sounded. He hoped that the low-light camera he'd webbed to the wall had gotten some shots that would be useful—as Defense Exhibit A at his trial, if nothing else. With the streetlights gone, the camera's usefulness now was a thing of the past.

Eddie laughed at him. "Everybody's seen more than enough of you already, Spider-Man. All I have to do is make sure you get captured at the scene of your crime."

"*I* didn't turn loose a bunch of hardened criminals on downtown Manhattan," Spider-Man said, as the flash of Connie Costaigne's camera cut through the darkness off to their right. Maybe the streetlights were gone, but that didn't mean that people weren't watching. "*You* did."

Stay close to him, Spidey reminded himself. Without a working spider-sense, if you lose this guy in the dark you'll never find him, and the last part of his trap will fall into place.

That was the depressing part about the whole thing. Venom had created the perfect frame. Spider-Man didn't have an alibi, he'd been seen and photographed at the scene by dozens of witnesses, his fingerprints were all over a load of stolen money—and all he had for a defense was a preposterous tale that would be useless unless he could bring in Venom to back it up.

The only thing left to do, then, was to grab hold of Venom and not let him go, regardless of appearances. It's time, Spidey thought, for me to commence beating seriously upon a seeming upholder of the law.

Reaching that decision was a great relief. No longer feeling the need to hold back, Spider-Man let fly with a massive punch that made Brock stagger under its impact.

"Let's get away from your pals," he said to

Brock as the punch went home, "and leave the police alone to clean up your jailbreak."

Brock recovered and kicked out, but the impact seemed light—at least, compared to Venom's usual pile-driver blows. Spider-Man wondered at the difference for a moment, and then understood. Just as Spidey had been holding back from the combat before, Brock was holding back now.

Brock didn't dare go all-out, Spider-Man realized. The moment he really let himself get into the fight, he would change into Venom—right in front of all the witnesses he'd called in to watch the "Downfall of Spider-Man Midnight Special."

I've got to make him mad enough to forget about his plans and turn Venom loose, Spidey thought. I know how to fight Venom—just get ready for some pain.

"Hey, Eddie, you know what?" he said as Brock grabbed him to deliver another punch. "I'm the one and only Spider-Man—*and you aren't.*"

Spider-Man whipped a web-line over Eddie's head. The line found an attachment point on the side of the abandoned bus bogged down in the drifts in front of the courthouse. He pulled on the extended web-line, dragging himself and Brock both over toward the stalled vehicle. The light from Castaigne's flash camera had come from that direction. She must have moved in daringly close, hoping for a better shot. If the name of the game now was "Put On a Show," the stranded bus would make an impressive stage.

"You wanted to finish me off," Spider-Man shouted as he and Brock together slammed against the side of the bus. Spider-Man's web-lines gave him the advantage. Without webs of his own, Brock was comparatively helpless. "Once I'm in jail, you'll never have another shot at my spleen," Spidey snarled. "So why not get the job done right now—if you're good enough take me down?"

"I *can* do it," snarled Brock. "And you *will* suffer!"

The snow muffled his words. The only light came from the strobing of Connie Castaigne's news camera. The flashes were irregular and disorienting, making freeze-frame pictures of blocky shapes and a haze of snowflakes suspended in mid-air.

Spider-Man put a wrestling hold on Brock and threw him into the side of the bus. Another flash came—still closer this time. Castaigne had moved dangerously close to the action in her quest for the perfect shot. Now Spider-Man saw a dark shadow sliding across Brock's face, and white fangs glistened in a horrifying grin as the camera strobed again.

"We have our webs now," Venom said. "We feel *good.*"

"Then come get me," Spidey said. Keep him angry, he thought—get Venom mad and keep him mad. Just do it without getting myself killed in the process. He vaulted to the top of the bus. "Hey, come get me!"

The next thing Spidey felt was the roof of the bus shudder as Venom landed on it. The top of the vehicle had been swept clean of snow by the howling wind, making it a clear—and conspicuous—place to fight.

A stage, Spidey thought. How wonderful. His moment of reflection was interrupted by a crashing blow to the head. He rolled with the blow and got back to his feet.

"At least I know where you are," he said aloud.

And at least he knew that Venom wasn't going to just vanish and leave him holding the bag, he thought. We're going to still be here locked in a struggle when the sun comes up.

"Your blood for my soup," Venom said, and leapt at Spider-Man.

Spidey dropped flat, letting Venom pass over, only to be roped with a loop of webbing that the super-villain dropped around him. Tied together, they rolled almost to the edge of the bus top before Venom managed to reverse

The next thing Spidey felt was the roof of the bus shutter as Venom landed on it.

their direction and push them back toward the center.

"Ha!" Spider-Man gasped, getting in punches whenever he could. "You still can't hurt me!"

The trick now was to keep Venom from thinking. The symbiote was tricky in his fighting rage, and full of a certain low cunning, but he didn't have the forethought and the tactical ingenuity of, say, a friendly neighborhood Spider-Man. As long as Venom didn't get a chance to use Brock's brain, he wouldn't remember that every moment he spent in his black-and-white, fang-snapping persona was a moment that worked to destroy his carefully worked out plan.

"Liar!" Venom screamed. A smashing blow from one of his fists caught Spider-Man in the bicep, numbing his whole arm. "There never was innocence in you. We *can* hurt you. We have before, and we will now. You're a liar, Spider-Man!"

"It takes one to know one," Spider-Man said, shaking some feeling back into his arm. He dropped to one knee and took aim at a nearby building with a web-line. "Any scrap of innocence you ever had is long gone, Venom."

Without his spider sense to warn him, Spidey had to rely on counting off seconds for a clue to his adversary's timing. When he got to the point in his count where he thought Venom would attack, he pulled on the web-line, lifting himself off the roof of the bus. A thud and an "Ooof!" from the roof told him that Venom had landed on the spot where he'd just been.

Spider-Man let go of the web-line and dropped feet-first onto Venom's back. "You're mine now. Don't try to run."

If he does the smart thing and runs, Spider-Man thought, then I'm in big trouble: left on the scene of the crime, with no super-villain in custody to prove my story. But Venom's blood was up, and the alien symbiote had no thought for anything but the violence at hand.

"Run from you?" Venom spun below Spider-Man, knocking him down. "Not in a million years!"

Now Venom was on top, pinning Spider-Man down onto the freezing metal of the bus top. Venom punched down. The lack of light was as much of a handicap to him as it was to Spider-Man—the blow only grazed Spider-Man's head, but even that was enough to daze him.

This is easy, Spider-Man thought over the ringing in his ears. He punched back blindly, and Venom's grip loosened enough for Spidey to wrench himself free of the pin. All I have to do is make it through the night. Only six more hours or so.

Six hours.

In close combat with Venom.

I must be nuts.

The strobing of the photographer's camera went on and on. Spider-Man realized that not all of those bursts of light were camera flashes. Some of them were the stars he was seeing every time Venom managed to land a punch. Those punches to the head had to be adding up.

Time for another risky move, Spider-Man decided. Let's play follow-the-leader.

He jumped, shot a web-line to the side of the courthouse, and swung himself upward.

"Coward! You can't leave yet!" Venom said, and moved after him in an instant.

Now came one of the most dangerous games of cat-and-mouse Spider-Man had ever played. He couldn't escape, but he couldn't let Venom catch him, either. As soon as the game ended, he would be ruined: disgraced on the one hand, or dead—minus his spleen and any additional organs that Venom might find tasty—on the other. The only safety lay in going on. The wind moaned mightily, the snow blew, and Venom, a black-and-white nightmare that never tripped his spider sense, was out there. Spider-Man had to keep Venom angry, keep him from remembering his plans, until it was too late.

Too late for me already, Spider-Man thought as he felt Venom's legs wrap unexpectedly around his waist. Where did he come from?

"Your spleen," Venom said. His clawed hands shot toward Spider-Man's midriff. "We want your spleen."

"Not just yet," Spidey said. He knocked the hands away and broke the leg grip. A mistake, maybe—without anything to hold him, he went flying unsupported through the howling air. In the snow-filled darkness, he had no way of telling up from down: no lights in the city, no moon in the sky, and the wind could be coming as easily from beside as from below him as he fell.

For a moment Spider-Man was utterly disoriented. But his spider senses came to his aid, giving him an intense awareness of approaching danger. The alarm couldn't be coming from Venom, so it had to be the ground. Over *that* way, and close.

His mental map of the area snapped back into place. Web-lines shot out, despite the wind, to cling to the icy face of a building. The first jerk on the line broke a sheet of ice away from the building, and he was falling again. Another web-line—another swing—and he was down, wallowing in the softly resistant cushion of a twenty-foot snowdrift.

For a moment he thought that his deadly game of tag had played itself out. But a second later, Venom dropped into the snow beside him. He could feel the human-alien symbiote's hot breath against his masked face.

"Here at last, the end," Venom said.

"Not yet," Spider-Man said. "You're going to have to work harder than that to get me."

"Get you? We already *have* you."

Venom grappled with Spider-Man. Wrestling in the snowdrift was like wrestling in cold, soft mud. It slowed them, chilled them, and dimmed their vision even more than the lack of streetlights.

Up and down they went, until, with a burst of flakes, they rolled out of the sheltering drift and back into the full fury of the storm.

Spidey threw a web-line high. It caught, and he followed it. He scrambled up the line, spinning in the wind. And whenever he looked, he saw Venom's grinning teeth right behind or beside him.

Down below, Spider-Man spotted another flash of the photographer's strobe. Connie Castaigne hadn't given up. Zero in on that, he thought. Give her the proof. Show the press that Venom was here, that Venom was the one

Spider-Man was fighting all along. Or even better—

—Even better, get Venom to reveal himself as Spider-Man, the *criminal* Spider-Man. No one would have to provide an alibi for the real Spider-Man, when he could create his own by showing the world a photo with two Spideys in the same frame.

It was perfect. The only hard part would be convincing Venom to go along with the idea.

From seemingly out of nowhere, Venom's fist smashed into Spidey's head.

Spidey tasted acrid blood in his mouth. Yeah, getting Venom to agree was going to be kind of tough.

CHAPTER 12

SPIDER-MAN WAS HURTING and exhausted, bruised and battered. Being alive but in jail had some real advantages over being dead, he was beginning to think.

They had tumbled back onto the top of the bus. It was cold and slick. Without the advantage of his spider senses, he couldn't avoid danger from Venom. Nor could he take much more of a beating before the monster made good on his threat. I'll take off and leave in five minutes, Spider-Man told himself. He who fights and runs away. . . .

No, that wouldn't work, either. He'd been called a coward before, and it hadn't felt good. Those other times, regardless of what some people said, his withdrawal had been tactical, not an admission of defeat. This time, it *would* mean defeat.

Just hold on another five minutes. I can do five minutes standing on my head.

More pain crashed through him as Venom attacked again from a direction Spider-Man didn't expect. "We know you better than you know yourself," Venom said. "You can't possibly win."

Spider-Man was about to admit that maybe Venom had a point when he spotted something in the air. At first it seemed like a moving dot, flickering in and out of sight. It grew closer, and took on a familiar shape. A flaming red, flying shape.

"The Torch!" Spidey exclaimed with relief.

"Don't try that old 'look behind you,' routine," Venom said. "It won't work." He threw a vicious kick at Spidey's mid-section.

"It's your plan that hasn't worked," Spider-Man said as he managed to roll under the blow. He felt a surge of renewed energy. Now that the Torch was on the way, he could hold out forever if he had to. "You've forgotten your plan."

"To eat your spleen? No, we remember that very well." Venom grinned, tongue lolling. "Eat your brain too, if we're hungry later."

"No, you wanted to discredit me first, remember? No one should see Venom here."

"Oh, you prefer fighting the police?" Venom's symbiote flowed and changed, shifting back to the fake police uniform.

"Yeah," Spider-Man said. He launched a web-line over Venom's head and swung around behind him, sweeping Venom's legs out from under him so that he smashed face-down onto the roof of the bus. "The thing I like best about your cop suit is that I can swing and you can't when you're dressed that way."

"Then look at us *this* way," Venom said. The symbiote morphed into a facsimile of Spider-Man's own costume, and Venom sprung back to his feet.

"Torch!" Spider-Man yelled. "Give him the works—now!" Spidey quickly threw an arm up to cover his eyes.

Hovering in the air above them, the Human Torch flared up to a painfully bright intensity, shining for a moment like a blazing star. The clear light illuminated the top of the bus, the snow around it—the entire scene.

I sure hope those folks from the Globe *got a shot of that,* Spidey thought. *Spider-Man versus Spider-Man, right there in the spotlight.*

The Torch faded back to his steady red flame. The intense heat had melted the thin layer of snow and ice on the top of the bus. The water was rapidly freezing again in the extreme cold.

"Grab him!" Johnny called. "Don't let him get away!"

The real Spider-Man grappled with the fake as Johnny Storm took the sonic gun—the same one Reed Richards had used to separate the symbiote from Spider-Man when Spidey first realized that the symbiote was trying to bond to him permanently—and aimed it at them both.

One of the two figures had his red-and-blue costume ripple and change to black, and Eddie Brock screamed in pain as his other was ripped from him. But the snow was deadening the sound of the sonic gun, reflecting it and diffusing it. The symbiote was only partially disrupted. It flowed back into place.

"That's not fair," Venom said. "But we don't care. Now comes the death of Spider-Man."

"Torch!" Spider-Man yelled. "Melt the snow!"

The Torch swooped down into the snowbank on the leeward side of the bus. As he had done while they were taking the homeless people to the shelter, he melted the snow to slush. Then he flew off, gaining altitude and getting into position for another shot at Venom.

"The sonic gun. Now!" Spider-Man said.

Again the powerful blast of disrupting sound shot forth. It flayed the symbiote from a part of Brock's body. At that moment, Spider-Man threw himself at Venom. They both fell from the bus roof into the giant puddle of slush beside it. Already a thin coating of ice glittered on top of the slush as the two superpowered beings crashed onto it.

Gathering his remaining strength, Spider-Man tore himself away from Venom, pushing the frantic symbiote back into the freezing liquid. Part of the symbiote, the part that was detached from Brock, was locked in the newly frozen ice.

"More sonics!" Spider-Man shouted.

A bit more of the symbiote came loose. Spider-Man knocked Eddie and his other back into the freezing slush. Cold water feels like fire to bare skin; hypothermia slows a man down both mentally and physically. Brock didn't escape the effect. And more of the symbiote was coated with ice.

Again and again Spider-Man and the Torch melted snow to create water, then used sonics to drive a bit more of the symbiote off into the freezing slush, where it was stuck, unable to extricate itself. Venom was trapped. The symbiote was caught in ice, and Eddie Brock—unprotected from the fury of the wind-lashed snow—was unable to tear free of the frozen pool to which he was bound.

"What kept you?" Spider-Man asked the Torch as they worked methodically to separate Venom into its component parts.

"More sonics!" Spider-Man shouted. More of the symbiote came loose. Spider-Man knocked Eddie and his other back into the freezing slush.

"The team from the Vault needed a bit of extra help," the Torch said. "With the flying weather being what it was, they couldn't be sure of getting here at all. I had to guide them in."

At that moment, with a sighing lurch, the Vault's super villain apprehension unit arrived in their heavy-lift helicopter. Seconds later it had settled on a flat-roofed court building. A strike team jumped out carrying a mobile containment pod. They quickly descended to the ground.

"Where's the perpetrator?" said the officer in charge of the Vault team.

"Over here," Spider-Man said He pointed at Eddie Brock. "He's a little chilly."

"Got him." The crew from the Vault set to work containing Eddie Brock and his symbiote—separately—and hauling them both away. Spider-Man turned back to the Torch with a sigh of relief.

"Is that it, then?" he asked shakily.

Johnny Storm stepped closer to the exhausted super hero, warming and drying him with a controlled burst of heat. "That's it, Spidey," he said. "Venom's back in custody . . . and you still have your spleen. What more could you want?" he added with a grin.

At that moment, another figure—this one on skis—detached itself from the shadows, and headed rapidly toward Spider-Man. Spidey saw, with only a faint sense of surprise, that it was Ben Urich. The *Bugle* reporter had found his news story in the snowstorm after all.

At the same time, Connie Castaigne and Bertie van Tahn came over on their snowmobile. "Hey, Ben," Bertie said. "I didn't know you knew how to ski."

"A good reporter learns whatever he has to," Ben replied. "What kind of slant are you guys putting on this story for the *Globe* tomorrow?"

"'Venom attempts to discredit Spider-Man,'" Bertie said. "How about you?"

"About the same," Ben said.

"Only I have photos and you don't," Bertie said. He gestured at Connie, who waved her camera at Ben triumphantly. "So we'll see who sells more papers. Later!"

And with that the two *Globe* staffers sped off.

"Think I can have an exclusive interview?" Ben said to Spider-Man as the snowmobile vanished in the blowing snow.

"Yeah, I think so," Spider-Man said. "But what are you going to do about pictures?"

"There's a kid, a freelancer," Ben said. "Maybe you've seen his byline on some photos? He comes in with some of the best super hero photos you've ever seen. My guess is that when I get back to the office, he'll be waiting with 8 x 10 glossies of this whole thing."

He pulled a voice-activated tape recorder out of his pocket and aimed it at Spider-Man's face. "Now tell me, when did you first learn that Venom was up to something?"

"I'll tell you that if you tell me how you came to be here yourself," Spider-Man said.

"A newsman never reveals his sources," Ben said, "but in this case I'll make an exception. A feature-writer from Brooklyn was calling everyone in town, telling them to come down here to see Spider-Man in action."

Ben glanced around. "Looks like the snow's finally easing up some. Now back to the story. What *was* it that first tipped you off?"

A while later, Peter Parker stood at the pay phone in the lobby of the *Daily Bugle*. He had Spider-Man's costume in his backpack, and he was holding the Fantastic Four's camera. He found a quarter in his pocket, slipped it into the telephone, and called home.

"Mary Jane?" he said when his wife picked up the phone. "I'm at the *Bugle*. I'm sorry, honey, but I'm going to be a little bit later getting home than I thought—first I have to develop some pictures of Spider-Man."